HEAVEN FOR A
PREDATOR

by
Ysadora Sonderling

For Ben, and your brutal honesty.
For Taylor Herring, and your brutal edits.

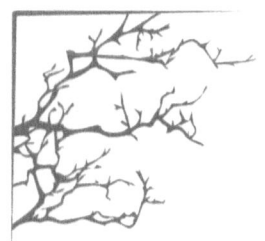

Chapter 1

Autophagia- the ultimate taboo in the world we created. The act of feeding upon oneself. See, in this world, things had nice clear delineations. You either lived or you didn't. You either fed or you starved. This world of black and white duality was often times bleak, but there wasn't much choice in the matter. This was-

Furii sighed and sat back against the wall. Writer's block hit like a bitch when you were trying to talk yourself up. She popped another blood capsule into her mouth and swallowed without breaking it. No matter how long she had been alive and infected, she never got used to the taste of blood. The caps kept her alive and helped her heal. That was it.

Frustrated, she put her notebook down and sat up, reaching for her comms pod. Tapping it once brought up the screen, already logged into the bounty hunter network. Checking her data lines revealed no new messages. This meant no new official work. She cursed under her breath before bringing up her bank accounts. Seeing the sorry state her finances were in made it clear that Furii was going to have to find a nest. Tapping the pod again snapped the screen shut, and she threw it down on the bed beside her.

Things had been tight before, but this was a new low. If she kept going like this, she wasn't even going to be able to afford ammo. This essentially meant that she was going to be out of business. She turned back to her advertisement. What was the best way to describe her area of expertise? How could she glamourise the role of a vampire bounty hunter? Come hire me or you will be 'phage kibble. Preserve the balance a little longer or your humans are chow. Just call Furii Hellstorm for all your pest removal needs.

There was no way of making it pretty, but she was a necessity. The vampires of myth and legend had turned out to be real, and with the population boom of the last millennium, well, more food meant more predators. Vampires had killed indiscriminately, and infected equally indiscriminately. They had become a plague, spreading across the world and wiping out almost everything with a circulatory system. The planet died too- most animals were eradicated, 99% of the plant population became extinct. Desert and wastelands were ubiquitous. Suddenly vampires discovered how lonely it was at the top of the food chain. When they started to starve, they finally got wise.

That was around 30 years ago. The humans became a protected species due to vampires needing them to live. Killing them became illegal, as did infecting them. Humans were cared for well, and they happily donated blood in exchange for protection against the population that had almost made them extinct. Well, comparatively speaking.

Unfortunately, not all vampires saw fit to fall in line with the laws. Some were relics of the old days and still attempted to feed directly from the humans They were hunted down and put to death by people far higher up on the food chain than Furii. In many of the regions that were the poorest, the vampires resorted to feeding from themselves or each other, an act of autophagia. This resulted in a twisting of their sanity, and autophages became something primal, a bestial creature. They were devoid of control and had limited intellect. Autophages were craven and baseless killers who fed off humans, vampires, or any living creature they could get their misshapen hands on.

Luckily for Furii, these beasties provided good business for her particular skill set. There was a general kill-on-sight order, with a cash reward for each confirmed kill. Bounties were placed on autophages who terrorised a particular community, and it was these jobs that paid the best. When the active bounties ran out, it was up to Furii to quite literally chase up new work. Alas, that was the point Furii had arrived at now. Tomorrow she would have to go searching for a new nest to retain her title of being the best in the business on this side of the country.

Taking up her notebook again, Furii picked up where she left off. She wrote and rewrote her advertisement well into the morning, finally just lying down and crashing out.

It was well into the early evening when Furii awoke, feeling a little better. She had something of a sensical advertisement to broadcast far and wide, and it would take the very last bits from her account. Hopefully the risk would pay off, and if not, she could always find more small fry.

Speaking of small fry she thought, it was time to go terrorise some more blood-addled suckers. She popped two blood caps in to get breakfast over and done with before heading for a shower. Her shitty little villa had a bathroom she could barely turn about in, but the fact that it had running water, which even warmed up at times, was a major selling point. She carefully shaved her head, leaving her long locks down the centre in place. This month they were shades of orange and red. It matched her eyes well. The water heater faltered for a second, running cold drips over every scar and burn on her dark skin.

Vampires could heal fast, but her line of work meant that she would scar up her skin as fast as she could heal it. The hot water eventually took mercy and kicked in again. Furii sighed happily as the cold tension was relieved and her wretched skin relaxed. There were plenty of occupational issues as a bounty hunter, most of which involved actively bleeding.

After showering and drying, Furii dressed tactical- dark denim pants, a black shirt, black body armour and a black leather motorcycle jacket. The body armour had been scavenged from one of her very first kills and was part of the reason why she was known as the best in the business. All she had to do was paint over the redundant camo with black paint. There was no use wearing camo when it was night and she was hunting nocturnal creatures.

As far as weaponry went, she had a modified crossbow used to shoot handmade stakes. This folded down and strapped at her hip, ready to be drawn and unfolded at a moment's notice. Several larger stakes were tucked into various places around her body, and her trusty pair of sickle blades sat on the other hip. When it came to 'phages, you could stake them or decapitate them, nothing more. Even amputated limbs eventually grew back, given enough blood and time. Not even vampires could manage that one.

A stake to the heart was widely known to be the best method of killing a vampire, but part of Furii's secret to success was something not known to the wider community. This was something passed down by the Hellstorm clan, from mentor to student. A stake anywhere other than the heart would not kill or even really maim a vampire, but if that stake was made from sacred wood, well, that was a different matter. When a vampire's blood came into contact with palo santo wood, a vicious reaction occurred. If they got so much as a splinter in a finger, it caused an uncontrollable burning sensation. It was much like using a stun gun on a human. The palo santo had the handy effect of incapacitating them until the hunter could come and finish the job. Of course, Furii was also a vampire, so she had to be very careful when creating her arsenal. She had felt its sting once before and had learnt the lesson well. Now she wore full gloves and even a face mask. You only pepper spray yourself once with palo santo.

To complete her gig, she strapped on her last line of defence, a wickedly large Colt .45. While shooting a vampire didn't kill them, punching a large chunk of blessed iron through their face certainly slowed them down. Sitting snugly in her thigh holster, the firearm was perfectly placed for drawing in a sticky situation. It shone like a new penny, polished to perfection.

Downing a few extra blood capsules gave Furii the much-needed energy kick for taking out a nest of autophages. Finally she retrieved the old metal tin with her precious tags in it. These tags were uniquely coded zip ties that had to be attached to each autophage she killed. Each tag was looped through the Achilles tendon and was a way to ensure that each 'phage that was paid out for was actually a new kill. In the early days a few unscrupulous individuals kept passing off the same phage as another kill. Some even grave-robbed the 'phages that had already been paid out. It was also a good way of keeping an eye on the activity of each bounty hunter. The sheriff's department dosed out the tags to all its bounty hunters. However, when it came to the actual hunting of autophages, the hunters were given total freedom as representatives of the law.

Placing the tin in her duffle bag meant that Furii was ready to start. It was time to hunt.

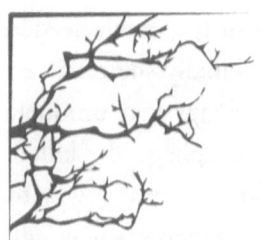

Chapter 2

F urii's vehicle was fully reinforced and had all the latest essential
modifications for the nighttime hunter. Not that she needed much
of it, but it was better than just having a measly set of headlights. It even
had a night vision and infra-red camera on it, for when she didn't want
to use said headlights. Being stealthy and all that. Autophages might be
clouded grey-eyed creatures, but they could certainly see headlights in
a desert wasteland.

It resembled more of a truck than a car, being an awkward and
bulky hunk of metal. The appeal lay in the fact that it was heavily
reinforced, and had enough space in the back to store at least 40
autophage bodies, and it was refrigerated. The modern-day tumbril,
removing the bodies of those the executioner had slain.

She was heading west; a bounty hunter rumour had it that were a
few nests on the edge of the wastes there. Close enough to pick at the
fringes of what passed for civilisation in this era, but far enough out
that they remained the ghoul beyond the ridge. The further you got
from the centre of the fortress city the vampires had built, the poorer
people were and the more likely they would fall to autophagia. Even
those within the walls turned regularly, and many bounty hunters made
their wage hunting in the slums. Poverty made monsters of us all.

She bore west for a good half hour before she spotted some
collapsed ruins off to the south. This was exactly what she had been
hoping for. Autophages liked to hide out in the basements of
abandoned buildings. They were incapable of creating their own
shelter. Much like a feral animal, they sought refuge from the sunlight

and other predators in derelict ruins. They still had the wherewithal to remain in packs, so they weren't totally devoid of intellect.

The vehicle slowed to a halt around two hundred metres from the first of the ruins in an effort to preserve the element of surprise. Furii grabbed her duffle bag and crossbow before locking up her death-mobile. Slinking up to the closest building, Furii kept it low and silent. An awkward shuffling and slurping noise confirmed that her hunch was correct. There would be death tonight.

Before entering the dark recesses of the skeletal building, she carefully touched each element she would need at hand- confirming that each stake was in place, her sickles ready to go at a moment's notice, her crossbow strung and modified bolt loaded. She was as ready as possible.

Stepping into the shadows cast by the moon, Furii appeared to melt from sight. As silently and coldly as the grave, Furii picked her way through the rubble.

A piece of wall jutted out at an odd angle, and the old floorboards beneath it showed signs of great wear. Many feet had shuffled through here and disappeared into the gloom beneath the fallen wall. This must be the opening to their bolt hole, probably the basement of the fallen building. The shuffling from below was still without urgency, so Furii knew they were yet to detect her. While her eyes were sharp in the lowest of lights, she knew that as much as she would be able to see them, they would be able to see her. This had to be done fast.

Creeping under the fallen wall, Furii dropped down into the basement. From the gloom ravenous shrieks burst forth, and silver gleams of luminous eyes revealed the autophages hidden within its recesses. Counting the pairs, Furii deduced that there must be at least four phages present, all now whipped up into a snarling rage. The autophages were as removed to Furii as rabid mutts were to the most dignified show-worthy purebred beast. Their skeletal bodies had a freakish strength to them. The pallid skin seemed to be stretched over their sinewy form, to the point of translucence. This husk had the texture of parchment, covered in pocks and festering boils. Every one of their teeth was pointed, indicative of their lack of finesse in feeding. These were creatures made to rend flesh and exsanguinate a body through sheer brutality.

In the crepuscular light, Furii could see them flexing their rakish claws. For long seconds they were all still, each assessing the other for intention and weakness. It was Furii who broke the stand-off, unleashing chaos. She ducked low, shooting the nearest autophage with her crossbow, the force of which knocked it back into the gloom. The second threw itself at her, snapping its vile teeth like a bear trap. She rolled with it, using the momentum of the autophage to flip it over herself. Furii staked it in the ribs as it flew over and hit the wall behind her like a rag doll.

The third and fourth autophages were either more astute or more timid, as both stood back rather than launching in for a desperate frontal attack. Furii attempted to load another stake into her crossbow, but it was knocked from her grasp as she was viciously grappled to the ground. By some mercy, she managed to hold onto the stake she had intended to shoot. These were much thinner and shorter than the usual ones, making them cumbersome to use by hand. As the jaw of the third autophage closed around her leather-bound arm, Furii desperately rammed the modified stake into the body of the feral beast. Missing the heart meant that it did not die immediately. Instead it recoiled in agony from the sacred wood contacting its accursed blood. Furii left it incapacitated as she drew her sickles, their wooden handles a comforting and familiar weight in her hand. The final 'phage was warily watching, shifting its weight from foot to foot. She glanced around the room, reassuring herself that there were no other nasty creatures waiting to slink out of the darkness to attack her anew.

The last critter standing began to duck and weave, preparing to attack and assessing the best way to do so. It snarled animalistically, all its previous personality distilled into pure aggression. Furii decided to swing first, hoping to surprise her opponent while it was still trying to plan its attack. She managed to catch the creature in the neck with the point of her blade. It gave out a yelp of pain that degraded to a savage growl.

Now the beast lost all control, and threw itself upon her. With its teeth snapping within millimetres from her face, Furii held it off with her right arm. With her free hand, she hooked the sickle around the autophage's neck and hacked the head clean off with a single sweep. As its steaming blood rained down upon her face, Furii resisted the urge to vomit.

To dislodge the decapitated autophage, Furii rolled to one side, flinging the body off into the gloom. She lay there for a moment, panting with exertion and the adrenaline rush of hunting. Now was not the time to get complacent, however, as the autophage she had staked earlier was still kicking. A quick glance around revealed that it was attempting to crawl off into the darkness. Furii walked up to it, placing the blades of her sickles on each side of its neck. She quickly decapitated it with both blades and let the body slump back onto the floor. Furii did not waste time when it came to death, a lesson she had learnt the hard way in her early years. Back when the idea of killing anything made her stomach queasy, Furii hesitated too long to strike and had almost lost her arm. When her mentor killed the beast, it had gnawed through a good chunk of the bone already. That scar was one of the few that stayed permanent.

Scanning the room, Furii searched for any more autophages hidden away. Nothing immediately sprang out to her, so she opted to walk the boundaries of the basement just to be sure the nest was emptied properly. Missing one would put a dent in her payout to the tune of one hundred bits.

As she was passing a large vent, a silver gleam caught her eye. Cursing silently, Furii drew her gun before gripping the bars of the vent and tearing them off the wall. In seconds she had the gun at point blank range, square in the centre of the forehead of an autophage. It was a young girl, she appeared to only be around twenty years of age, with tiny wisps of blonde hair and huge doe eyes. Her teeth were pointed, and she was not snarling but... smiling. Furii paused a moment, caught off guard. Her finger twitched on the trigger; the urge to kill, to complete her lawful task was challenging her hesitation. Autophages were to be exterminated on sight, no grey areas. It was the reason why they were becoming rarer, and why the role of bounty hunter was becoming a dying art.

The autophage just stood there, completely still and oddly serene. Her long and clawed fingers trembled slightly as she looked down the barrel of the weapon pointing directly at her.

'Please, no.'

Those two words shattered Furii's resolve. Autophages were not meant to talk.

Autophages did not talk.

Autophages did not reason.

'What are you?' she asked suspiciously.

'What? I am like the ones you killed,' replied the doe-girl.

'No. Autophages cannot talk or reason. They just kill,' Furii snapped, angered by her own confusion.

'I can. I can communicate perfectly well, but I cannot kill. It is repulsive.' The girl shivered slightly when she spoke of killing, but Furii was unconvinced.

'There is a shoot to kill on all 'phages. Sorry, but this is what the law dictates. You cannot be allowed to leave here alive,' Furii said dutifully. The doe-girl began to shiver harder, fear wracking her body in great tremors. Her silver eyes became impossibly wide.

'If... if you must, my name is Isabel. Put that on my grave, legally-sanctioned murderer,' said the stroppy autophage, squaring off against Furii.

A second passed as Furii contemplated the gall of this girl, this Isabel.

Isabel.

Autophages did not have names.

Autophages did not have identities.

Isabel.

This creature was clearly cognisant of the world around her, of the danger Furii represented, and was trying to reason with her. This entire situation was highly unusual. There was nothing in the play book about sentient autophages and what to do with them. She hesitated, then lowered her weapon.

'I am calling this one in. Sheriff's department will want to know about this. Siddown.' Furii gestured to a busted chunk of wall that would work as a seat for now. Isabel nodded sadly, sitting down obediently at the serious end of a gun. Furii made a quick check of the room to make sure there were no other hidey holes. When she was satisfied that there were no more surprises awaiting her, she pulled out her comms pod to call the sheriff's department about Isabel. She was greeted with a blank screen and nothing but static.

Cursing the lack of reception out in the wastes, Furii looked at Isabel, who was still sitting down, those huge eyes fixed upon her. Gesturing for Isabel to stand, Furii decided to march her out of the basement and try calling again above ground. Unwilling to have an autophage behind her, despite how reasonable it may seem, Furii motioned towards the opening with her gun.

'Gotta call in above ground. Move it!' she snapped gruffly.

'Oh, okay. I'm sorry if you-'

'Just move.'

The autophage complied, jumping out of her seat and creeping through the main room of the basement. Furii kept her gun pointed at the girl's back, still wary of this anomaly. Shuffling through the bodies of the slain autophages, the girl looked sadly at the remains. Furii grunted the question to her.

'They were my family. Father, mother, sister, random creepy uncle. Well, mentally they had been gone for years, but they still were... mine,' sniffled Isabel. Furii grunted again, feeling uncomfortable about the teary psychotic killing machine before her. Nodding sadly, Isabel moved towards the entrance of the basement area, scrabbling wildly to get through the opening without help. She was such a scrawny kid, it seemed as though her twig-like arms could snap at any moment. Finally, she popped through, falling in a heap on the shifting sands. Furii shouted up from below.

'No funny business now y'hear? You sit your rickety bones down up there.'

'Yes miss.' The sarcasm was thick.

As much as the use of 'miss' rankled her, Furii chose to ignore it, instead focusing on extracting herself from the nest.

When she was topside, Furii looked around carefully as there may yet be more autophages out there in the gloom. When nothing surfaced, she pulled out her comms pod again. Connecting to her beloved truck, Furii used the pod as a remote control. She drove the truck up to the edge of the ruins and opened up the back of it.

'Sit.'

'You are real talkative you know. I haven't had a conversation in at least 3 years, now I get stuck with a monosyllabic...' Big-eyed Isabel stopped talking abruptly when she saw the furious look on her captor's face. 'OK, I get it. No talking. Don't bond with the prey before you kill it right?' she said, in an effort to antagonise Furii.

'Just sit down.' Furii snapped at the girl, taking the bait. She was even more annoyed that the autophage was showing personality. Just another weird part of a weird day. Finally the girl sat, and Furii could get on with making her call. This time her comms pod sprang into life.

She dialled up the sheriff's office. An apathetically gruff voice answered after a few rings.

'Sheriff's department, what's the problem?'

'This is hunter 4095, Furii Hellstorm.' She reported.

'Hellstorm clan? You lot never call in,' said the rough voice on the other end, their surprise evident.

'Normally don't need to,' Furii answered, dodging around the fact that almost every 'problem' was handled in-house.

'Well, shoot.' The officer on the phones tonight was clearly eloquent.

'I am clearing out a nest in the west sector, approximately 18 miles out, and I found a... Well, I found a talking autophage. It is completely in control and capable of rational communication. What does the department do in this kind of situation?' The person on the other end of the line fell completely silent and waited until Furii was done.

'Sounds like the sheriff will want to have the final decision on this one. Hold a moment please.' The voice on the line was replaced by jarring, jangling music. Furii swore loudly.

'Great, the world has gone to hell, but we still have abysmal hold music. You, Isabel. Stop touching things!' Furii snapped as she noticed the girl poking around inside the truck.

'Sorry. I was just wondering how many of my kind you have thrown in here. Not that they weren't lost... but when the time comes, will you just throw me in there too? Like all the broken ones?' Isabel shot back before dropping her head and fiddling with some loose pieces of rope in her hands. Furii opened her mouth to give her outraged response, but the discordant music in her ear stopped abruptly and an even gruffer voice answered.

'I am told ye have a freak on the hunt?' said the voice, which Furii had to take on faith as being the sheriff.

'Uh, yes. I came upon an autophage who exhibits speech and free will. She is totally aware, and not feral like the others.'

'How do you know it's an autophage then? It is probably some poor little vampire girl, held by those creatures. She must be terrified,' he patronised, using an almost childlike voice.

'With all due respect,' said Furii, meaning absolutely no respect for this condescending faecal cake,' she looks exactly like an autophage. Excess canine dentition, sallow skin, clawed fingers. Short of genetic testing, that's an autophage.'

'Ugh, how vile. Well, how can you tell it is capable of thought? It is probably just mimicking things.'

'For one, she introduced herself to me, then chastised me for apparently murdering her family,' said Furii, beginning to really lose her temper at the questions and insinuations levelled at her. Isabel looked on with pure interest at the one side of the conversation she could hear. Furii glared at her, this little spanner in the works.

'I see. Well, it looks like an autophage, kill it. It's too ugly to keep alive. Tag it as usual and problem solved,' responded the sheriff...Furii nodded quietly before clearing her throat.

'Uh, yes I shall,' she said, an odd feeling making her throat constrict, although she couldn't place what it was. Feelings of this nature were foreign to Furii, ever confident in her general understanding of the world as it had been for over one hundred years. She tapped the comms pod and severed the link to the sheriff. Turning to Isabel, a grim glare darkened her face.

'Stand up. Over there.' Furii pointed to a sandy patch a few steps away. She wasn't about to get weird autophage blood on her truck. The kid stood up, glaring at Furii with her milky grey eyes.

'Bad news for me huh? Guess they don't want a 'freak' messing up their perfect world. Gonna blow my brains out into the sand? Bag and tag me like my sister?' snapped Isabel, feeling a little argumentative about the entire situation.

'Just move. Kneel!' Furii hissed, disliking the way this night was panning out. Isabel smirked and marched over to the sand as ordered.

She kneeled, staring Furii dead in the eyes. Placing the razor sharp blades of her scythes around Isabel's throat, Furii mentally prepared herself for the execution. She reminded herself again and again that this was not only legal, it was obligatory.

Furii paused for three long seconds, with the blades a deadly weight in each hand. She tensed, flexing to gain the strength and speed needed to complete her deadly task. All the while, Isabel looked up at her, her grey eyes meeting Furii's red ones. Furii snarled like a feral animal, but stayed her hand. Withdrawing the blades, she stomped angrily over to her truck. Fishing around in the back for something to help her restrain Big Eyes resulted in a handful of standard zip ties. She looped a few together to form a longer tie and turned back to Isabel. Taking the kid's tiny hands, Furii bound them quickly with the ties and led her to the front of the truck.

'Wait, what are you doing? I thought the sand would be red with my blood right now. As well as your hands,' said Isabel curiously as her eyes poured over Furii's face.

'Don't get too excited. I am taking you to the sheriff. People need to know if there are different... people need to know.'

'Your sheriff ordered me dead, I don't think they care. They are as likely to kill me there anyway, or do some kind of horrific scientific experiments,' Isabel stated flatly.

'Well... its the law.' Reiterated Furii, trying to convince herself it was right. Isabel opened her mouth to argue again but Furii shoved her onto the floor of the truck and slammed the door. Cursing loudly, she went to collect her prize bodies.

5

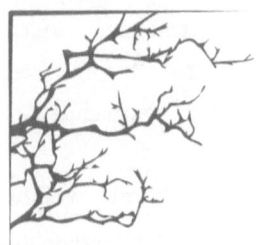

Chapter 3

When all four dead autophages had been dragged from the nest, tagged and thrown into the back of the truck, Furii climbed into the cab. She opened her stash tin and threw a few blood capsules into her mouth to begin the healing process. Although she had bested the autophages, there were still myriad bruises and scratches adorning her skin. As always, Isabel watched her closely. Before she could say anything, Furii hissed at her loudly.

The truck roared into gear as Furii planted her foot and accelerated away. Dust plumed behind the vehicle as she began the drive home. The kid was smart enough not to speak, but eventually wriggled her way up onto the seat beside Furii. When the sickly yellow city lights had broken the horizon, Furii's comms pod chimed loudly. She stopped the truck's relentless march and activated the call.

'Hellstorm, is it dead?' barked the voice of the sheriff.

No...' Replied Furii, keeping guarded.

'Why not? It must be killed before you reach the city. Kill it now,' ordered the voice.

'Why is it so important that it be done now? This autophage isn't feral, so why should it- she be put to death? What if she is the answer to the autophagic plague?' asked Furii, genuinely confused about this extreme stance.

'Look, it's just a 'phage. Do your job, kill it and get your reward. It's too ugly to matter anyway.' Furii could almost see the spittle coming from the sheriff's twisted mouth as he spoke such hate-filled words. Furii had only met him a handful of times, but she could imagine the vile man speaking such words perfectly. She remained silent, so he continued.

'Failure to bring in a bounty, especially one the sheriff personally knows about, is an offence. As the sheriff, it is up to me to set the punishment for insubordination. Kill the creature or I will personally ensure you lose everything,' he spat, and abruptly ended the call. Furii sat there silently, her ears ringing with the hatred of the law. Ordinarily she wouldn't think twice about killing an autophage, but seeing a sassy young girl with enough sentience to insult her had Furii second-guessing her resolve. Still, it was not worth losing everything over.

'Yes sheriff, I will complete the hunt,' murmured Furii before cutting the call and tapping her comms pod shut. She gripped the steering wheel tightly, watching the blood drain from her knuckles. Isabel decided to break the silence.

'Your people really hate mine. If it were anything but autophages it would be a genocide. It seems like we are just animals to you. Well, for what it's worth, I want to live,' she said to Furii, who sat quietly and pondered her options. Her night was starting to absolutely stink. Throwing open the door in anger, Furii jumped out of her truck, raising massive plumes of dust. Furii stared at the night sky. It should be so easy.

Get the autophage.

Kill the autophage.

Get paid.

Simple.

She stalked around to Isabel's door, looking again at the city. Streaks of light began to sully the sky in the east. She was losing time. The door to the passenger side was jerked open. Isabel stared out at Furii, her storm cloud eyes sullen.

'Gonna blow my brains out in front of your pretty city with all its shining lights?' she asked testily.

'It's hardly pretty, and the lights only show the scum better. Get down,' Furii snapped in return. Isabel acquiesced and awkwardly slid down as her hands were still bound. She flinched as Furii snatched up one of her smaller knives.

With a single move Furii grabbed the autophage's wrists and pulled her closer. Isabel closed her eyes. For once no irritating comment passed her purple lips. With a snarl Furii cut her bindings, throwing them into the truck.

'Go, get out of here.'

'But aren't they expecting to see my body?' Isabel blurted out before she could catch herself. She did not want to encourage the production of her dead body.

"You let me worry about that. You said you had a sister, I will tell them that is you,' Furii responded as the idea came to mind. Isabel shivered.

'But the sun is rising. I need you to drop me back there or I will have no shelter,' pleaded the girl.

'Oh no, they track the bounty hunter vehicles. If I go back they will know that something is wrong. Plus, I won't get back in time for the light curfew. You are on your own, kid,' Furii responded, slamming the passenger side door closed. Isabel looked utterly shocked.

'But out here I will die as soon as the sun comes up. You might as well kill me now. Death by sun is the worst way to go. Just kill me now thanks, *murderer*.' Isabel was passionate, her fervent words whistling around and through her pointed teeth. Furii motioned towards the desert. 'Can't you just take me... in there?' Isabel motioned instead towards the city.

'No way in hell. I cannot take you into the city, are you insane?' Furii was now incredulous at the audacity of this beast. They glared at each other for long minutes. The stand-off was broken by Furii huffing loudly and stamping her way to the rear of the truck. Isabel followed, curious as to the plan of this highly unusual vampire.

With the back doors open, Isabel looked sadly at her family. The mound of grey flesh barely resembled them, her proud father, plain but practical mother and her perpetually squabbling sibling. Even the uncle. Furii began to rearrange them without ceremony. When she had cleared an Isabel-sized space, Furii grunted and jerked her thumb towards it.

'Get in.'

'What?'

'Get *in*. This is the only way I can get you into the city.'

'You know what? I think I am good with the sun,' Isabel snapped back at Furii.

'Just get in the back and lie down. The only way I can sneak you into Morgisburg is if they think you are already dead. The city guards find autophages repulsive and that may be our ticket in. Please,' Furii added at the end, softening her stance. She was asking a lot of someone who looked to have barely left childhood. Isabel caught this empathy, and looked dolefully up at the older vampire.

'Yes, I will do this. Please... don't let them kill me,' she pleaded, those grey eyes almost blue in the growing dawn light. Despite the constant bravado, this kid wanted to live. She lay amongst her family, and Furii carefully covered her over with various limbs. Huffing in exasperation after she closed the door, Furii stamped over to the cabin. The engine fired up equally angrily and they rolled towards the mighty gates protecting the city and its occupants.

Upon approaching, the black-clad city guards stepped forward from the gatehouse.

'Bounty hunter 4095 returning from a fishing expedition. Autophages in the rear.' Furii repeated the same words she said every time she returned to the city and waited for the same checks to be done. The guards went around the vehicle with large mirrors on wheels, checking the undercarriage. When they were content there were no stowaways there or on the roof, they turned their attention to the internal parts of the vehicle.

'Opening the rear,' shouted one guard as they popped the back doors open. Furii's breath hitched in her throat as she prayed that Isabel would not move. It could very well mean both of their lives if she did.

'Ugh, they are even uglier than ever. Close the door and remove this foulness. What a stench.' One of the guards sounded like he was about to lose his lunch. What a pity someone had left a severed head staring back at them from atop the pile of limbs. Furii grinned, nodding back as they gave her the 'all clear' signal. She pulled away, making a beeline for her home rather than the sheriff's station. Pulling into her underground garage, Furii waited until the door was fully closed again before she stepped out of the cabin and opened the back. Luckily her little villa connected up to the garage, and she could sneak Isabel in without a soul seeing.

'That was revolting, but thank you,' said the kid. Tears slid down her dirt-stained face, taking some of the blood of her family with it. Furii nodded awkwardly and patted her on the shoulder.

'Come on, you need a shower, sustenance and a sleep.' The words came gruff and clipped as she showed Isabel the way into the villa. Giving a short tour, Furii emphasised the location of the bathroom before ducking off to change her clothes. Ordinarily she wouldn't bother to do so to just sign in, but she knew it was likely that they would be tracking her vehicle today. She even scrubbed her face.

Grabbing some extra blood caps for Isabel, Furii found her perched awkwardly on the couch.

'Here, take these. I don't need you going hungry in the middle of suburbia. I have to go check in or they will be hunting me down next,' she muttered and stalked out before Isabel could give a response.

The autophage stared after her, a combination of wonderment and uncertainty across her face.

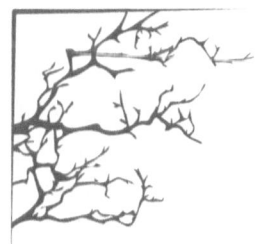

Chapter 4

As she backed out of her garage, a message came through her comms pod. It was an urgent request from the Duchess Du Mort, one of the most powerful vampires in one of the most corrupt families of the city. Her curiosity piqued intensely, Furii was irritated that she had to press on rather than find out what sort of lucrative morsel was on offer.

Furii drove over to the sheriff's building as fast as the law would allow, rehearsing her explanations and praying she could pull off this deadly little stunt.

Sunlight was beginning to stream across the sky now, so Furii was forced to drive using the daytime precautions. It was through the many fitted cameras that she saw the six heavily-armed officers waiting for her in the car park and loading dock of the Sheriff's Department. As she pulled in, they surrounded the car, guns levelled at her. She stopped short of the rotund vampire standing with his fat arms crossed over a grease-stained sheriff's uniform.

'Bounty hunter 4095, Furii of the Hellstorm clan. Is the beast dead?' he bellowed, the hate echoing around the concrete. Furii instinctively put her hands up as one of the armed and armoured vampires moved to open her door.

'It's in the back, decapitated. One of four.' Silent pleading became a mantra as they opened the back door. The sheriff indicated for the nearest vampire crony to keep pointing his automatic rifle at Furii, while the sheriff walked around to the back of the vehicle. Exclamations of disgust were heard, but Furii could gather nothing of whether they believed her or not. They began to unload the bodies.

'Hellstorm. Get back here and show me which one.' The direction was little more than a grunt, but Furii heard it just fine. The man with the rifle levelled at her used it to gesture for her to get out, a movement that gave her far greater fear as he kept his finger on the trigger. Still, she had little choice, and slithered out of her seat. The bodies had been laid out on the ash-grey concrete floor. They had been thrown down, a complete lack of dignity for the vampires they once were. Furii walked over to the corpses, no particular emotion readable in her severe countenance.

'This one. This is the one that talked,' she said evenly, trying to ignore the fact that each of the heavies still had their guns trained on her. The sheriff glared at her, beads of sweat running down his acne-scarred face. He looked like a balloon fit to burst, red and shiny, with every feature stretched out. The tension grew between them.

'You sure?'

'Yes, I decapitated it on the sand of the wastes, exactly as you commanded me.' Furii responded carefully, hoping to gently fluff his ego.

'Then why did you stop at your home for twelve minutes and fifty-six seconds, when you were ordered to present immediately?' he barked angrily. So they had tracked her. Time to try a new tactic.

'Well, see this one here? Splattered bits of filth all over me. This one sprayed me with blood. You know how vile these beasts are, I had to wash off the repulsive muck. Surely you understand how disgusting they are Sir?' Furii answered and waited as the sheriff worked his jaw and stared. The tension was crippling, long seconds dragging by with six guns all levelled at her and a twitchy sheriff. Finally the sheriff broke the stagnant scene.

'Right, the foul pests. Take out the trash boys, I will talk to our new friend upstairs.' The sheriff had barely finished talking when the guards put on their safeties and shouldered their guns. They began to drag away various body parts as Furii followed the sheriff to the elevator.

Together they rode down a floor and the sheriff showed her to his office. He threw his considerable girth behind his desk and fired up a full comms unit.

'I am glad you now see it my way, Hellstorm. These vermin skulk around our city and more join them every day. The citizens are afraid of the autophage plague for good reason. They are the scourge of our existence,' ranted the Sheriff, his face becoming a fascinating shade of crimson.

'What about the talking ones, what's that all about?' queried Furii, infinitely aware of the need for delicacy. The sheriff cast her a pointed look, and Furii tried to look as innocently curious as possible. With her ferocious exterior, she was not sure it was working, but she had to try. Finally the man grunted like a dissatisfied pig and responded.

'We have had a few reports over the last few years. All seemingly random. They were all put down regardless.'

'But what if they could be the solution to the autophage issue?'

'Nah. We don't permit those ugly *things* to live. They need to remain what they are. A feral animal to be hunted, and for the main population to be afraid of. People need the boogeyman to keep them safe and distracted. It is for their own good to be afraid; they stay within the city walls and listen to authority. It is for their own good like sheep with the wolves at the gate. They stay obedient and protected. I know you understand this.' He proselytised from behind his filthy desk, full of congealing mugs and confidential papers stained with food. Furii was disgusted by this man, this revolting example of vampirehood.

'Absolutely. It is better this way.' She kept it simple to avoid his suspicion.

'Exactly. Plus, what could be better than popping off a few extra vermin, right? I envy you bounty hunters. You get to be on the road, no laws, taking out the trash and getting paid to do it. Heaven!' Her impression of the sheriff was worsening by the second.

'I was adopted by the Hellstorm clan, didn't have much of a choice in the matter.' Furii explained as the sheriff sneered in distaste. Clearly this was a man used to pithy agreements.

'Well let's sort out your remuneration then. That is four autos at one hundred bits each, let's add another one thousand six hundred bits for your exclusive discretion. I authorise two thousand bits to be transferred to your account,' the sheriff thought aloud as he tapped away on his comms unit. Furii was so shocked that her voice came out as an unintelligible croak. Two thousand bits. That was a good three months of work at least. That was twenty autophages. Every time you went out, you weren't guaranteed to get a single autophage- some days you lost money. But here were the next few months, all wrapped up.

'Thank you... sir.' Furii struggled to term this puerile lump of vamp with any kind of respect. 'I will have to get home soon to avoid the sun.'

'Yes. Remember to keep your mouth shut or my boys will be visiting that little villa of yours,' he said by way of dismissal. There was no attempt made to hide that threat in the slightest. Furii didn't even bother responding, she just scampered to the elevator.

When she returned to her truck she discovered that it had been thoroughly searched in her absence. Whether this was by order of the sheriff or simply on a whim of the goons, Furii had no idea. She did notice that her stash of blood caps had gone missing, although the tin was thrown back onto her passenger seat. She huffed angrily and jumped into the cab.

The sun was now high enough to burn any vampire instantly. This had definitely been a late finish for Furii, and the deserted roads reflected this. Luckily she made it back into her garage without incident. As she placed the truck in park, Furii gave a deep sigh, releasing the pent-up tension of a night gone truly bad.

Upon entering her living room, Furii was witness to another sight. There was blood all over the coffee table and floor. In the congealed mess were many gnawed blood capsules all emptied of their precious bounty. Isabel sat in the middle of it all, covered in blood and shreds of the fibrinogen used to make the capsules.

'You really are hopeless, aren't you?' Furii sighed again. Isabel just smiled awkwardly, unable to think of an appropriate response. 'Look, just go and have a shower. I will clean this up.'

Isabel stood up quietly and walked into the bathroom, but Furii did not hear the water start. Even by the time she had finished sopping up all the blood, it was clear Isabel had not gotten into the shower. Furii walked towards the bathroom, noticing that she had even left the door open.

'Are you showering or... what?' Furii was astounded to see Isabel now standing naked and shivering in the middle of her bathroom, staring at the shower compartment. The autophage slowly looked up with her sad rain-cloud eyes.

'S- s- shower?' She spoke through chattering teeth. Furii resisted the urge to smack her own forehead. She turned on the console and helped Isabel into the water. She grabbed Isabel's clothes, which had been fashioned from makeshift rags, to throw in the bin. Come to think of it, autophages usually didn't have the wherewithal to care about clothing.

'Don't forget soap,' she muttered, handing the kid the bottle.

A few cold water hits and subsequent yelps later, Isabel was showered and dressed in some of Furii's old clothes. Furii settled her in to sleep on the couch before going and showering the weird night away. As she lay in her own bed, Furii pondered her bizarre day. This was definitely not how she had planned it going. The loud snoring coming from her living room was almost soothing, and Furii was soon lulled to sleep.

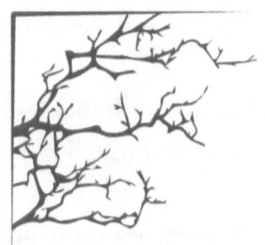

Chapter 5

The night broke, and Furii slept on. The lateness of the night before meant that she had to cut into the next night's hours in order to heal. When she finally started to wake, it was close to midnight already. Pondering all that had gone on in the prior evening kept Furii in bed until one in the orning. This strange little autophage felt important somehow, yet Furii knew she had to release it... her, as soon as she was able to smuggle her out of the city. To be caught actually housing an autophage was unheard of, but she was sure the punishment would be severe.

Furii's comms pod beeped quietly, shattering the silence and forcing her to focus back into the moment. She tapped it open and found a follow-up message from the Duchess Du Mort, curtly inquiring why Furii had not responded when her first message was so urgent. Furii swore under her breath and responded quickly. A volleyed message gave the address to the Du Mort mansion and an order to be there within the next half an hour. Tapping her comms pod closed, Furii launched herself out of bed. Padding into the kitchen, Furii opened a new pack of blood caps, seeing that most of hers had been stolen or gnawed on. She filled up her tin and put enough aside for breakfast for the two of them. Isabel began to get restless on the couch, her incredible hearing picking up on Furii's movements. She soon joined Furii in the kitchen.

'Here, take these. The capsule is totally edible for us, made from platelets and fibrinogen. You can crush them in your mouth or swallow them whole,' Furii explained, handing her the blood capsules.

'Oh, I thought you had to open them. We didn't have these when I... lived in a city,' Isabel explained. Considering that blood caps had been around for the last hundred years, Isabel had to be far older than Furii initially thought. Calling her 'kid' now seemed to be a little redundant.

'Well I have to get dressed. I would take you back out there, but I have an urgent meeting with one of the most powerful vampires in the city. She will not take any further delays. So you will have to sit tight again today,' Furii explained in between swallowing her capsules. Isabel nodded, then looked at the living room as her face lit up.

'Can I read your books? 'she asked excitedly. 'I remember books. They were my favourite thing. I want to read again.' Mystified by her enthusiasm, Furii nodded her permission. She bolted off towards the bookshelf with a skip in her step.

Retreating to her bedroom, Furii changed into a suitably respectable clan Hellstorm uniform to visit vampire aristocracy. The bizarre little autophage now tearing up her living room would have to wait. Urban legend had it that the Duchess would have any source of minor inconvenience killed if she so felt the need. Furii did not want to be the one to confirm that myth.

Pulling up to the colossal iron gates that isolated the Du Mort estate, Furii flashed her ID. The guards nodded but still checked over her entire vehicle in the same way the city guards did. Rather than checking for autophages that had stowed away, Furii was sure it was to ensure no poor people entered. Given the go ahead, the gates effortlessly opened. The rich certainly lived a very foreign life to Furii. She drove by vast green swathes of gardens, saw real flowers for the first time in decades, watched water just flung into the air. Between the sandy wastes and the grimy concrete of the city, this was an alien landscape to her. All of this scenery was lit up with so many lights it was impossible to miss a detail; vampires who live to spite the night, instead making it appear day.

From the gate to the house itself was a 5 minute drive alone. Furii was stunned when she finally did see the home. It was incomprehensibly large. Great wings extended from either side of the main hall, and rather unusually, the walls had windows. Rather than have to shutter their houses every day, most vampire dwellings simply did away with windows. Apparently, the rich required them. They did have extensive grounds to look upon.

Furii parked the truck directly in front of the main entrance. She could feel the inconvenience that her beaten up and bloodstained vehicle was causing to those glaring down from the windows above. Almost as soon as she had stepped out of the cab, Furii was joined by a suitably bland butler. He was impeccably dressed, not a hair out of place on his mostly bald head and not a single scuff on his responsible black shoes. This butler had snooty down to a rapturous art.

'Her Grace is expecting you. Allow me to take you to the drawing room where she is taking guests. Leave all weapons here.' At the last comment, Furii put her hands up, showing she had no weapons. The Hellstorm clan had very specific rules about expected decorum around their elite clients. They were well-renowned for discretion and reliability. Furii still had no particular idea as to why she had been requested for this job, however. With her long dreadlocked hair and dark skin, she seemed like the least appropriate choice from Hellstorm HQ. The butler looked her up and down, nodded and walked inside without another word.

The inner parts of the mansion were a rabbit warren of beige and damask. The front foyer alone was bigger than her entire villa. Furii managed to at least not gape in awe at the surroundings. Music played in many of the rooms and a variety of maids circulated constantly. There was even some kind of perfume being continuously piped into the rooms, something far too floral for Furii's tastes. Finally they approached a rare closed door. Even a standard interior door was ornate, covered in gilded flourishes.

Raised voices could be heard from within, followed by something shattering. The butler did not miss a beat, nor blink, nor react in any way. He rapped curtly on the door. There was a small flurry of activity before another man opened the door, bearing a broken vase and glass. He quickly excused himself and scurried off through the halls, red faced and hair akimbo. Furii looked to the butler with a questioning glare, but he refused to make eye contact.

'Your Grace, the requested representative from the Hellstorm clan has arrived,' he said with a flourish and a bow before quickly retreating. The Duchess Du Mort was surprisingly young, seeming as though she was in the human range of early 30s. Brown hair piled atop her head, an elaborate dress with a respectable neck and hemline, the Duchess could not be any more different from Furii. The rose-coloured dress even matched and enhanced the colour of her eyes. Rubies glittered on every finger, dripped from her ears and glorified her thin white neck. Furii felt instantaneously inadequate, which was clearly the idea.

'You, you are the best Hellstorm has to offer? Ugh. Their standards have dropped. People of... your type. Regardless, I have need of a bounty hunter. I have recently had a theft occur and you must retrieve my goods.' Her voice was arrogant and vapid.

Appropriately so.

'OK, what am I retrieving and who took it?' Furii asked, erring on the side of simplicity in her dealings with aristocracy.

'A... feeding human has been stolen, or someone helped them abscond. They also managed to make off with some valuables, though nothing of any real importance. I mostly wish for the human to be returned. If you find my items with him and return them, you will be given a bonus. I believe whoever took my human also took an emerald necklace and bracelet from my foyer, and a vehicle from my garage. All have been missing since.' The Duchess also chose her words unnervingly carefully. Furii's suspicion was piqued.

'How do you know that your human didn't just steal these things and run off?'

'I do not know it, however it is unlikely. The humans were... stored very well. No, I am sure this was an external robbery.' Her red eyes narrowed as she spoke. The Duchess was unaccustomed to being doubted.

'OK, can I see where this human was taken from, and information on the vehicle that was missing?'

'You can only see the outside of their lodgings. The humans are greatly upset by these events and keep to themselves. They will not leave their vigil, nor allow anyone in.' That last comment was oddly emphasised. Furii noted this inflection but did not respond.

'Well, I better just look at the outside then,' she agreed meekly.

Duchess Du Mort rang a small bell loudly. The butler reappeared within seconds.

'Yes, your Grace?'

'Show this Hellstorm to the outside of the... human lodgings, then show them the garage and describe the missing car. Go.' She dismissed them both with a wave of her hand and without wasting a word on niceties.

The butler nodded and sniffed, signalling for Furii to leave the room. She acquiesced, sensing the tension in the air and understanding the need to put up and shut up. She was in their world now. She was a complete foreigner.

The large building that housed the humans was singular in its blandness. Walls, windows, roof. Beige. It stood in stark contrast to the excess in the rest of the estate. The butler showed her the front door that had been kicked in; they walked a lap of the building, but there was really very little to be found. Furii stopped a moment, pressing her hand to the wall as if she were adjusting her boot. Instead she felt for those little flares of life, the pulses of the humans within. Interestingly, rather than feeling the rapid pulse of grieving or fear, she detected very slow pulses, more so than even a sleeping human. These were not terrified humans that had barricaded themselves in. The whole situation was getting weirder and weirder.

When the butler led her to the garage it was clear that another reinforced door had been kicked in. The massive expanse within the building was covered in mahogany and gold inlay, mother of pearl and ebony. The floors were spotless despite the vehicles. Specialised down-lights illuminated each sparkling panel of steel perfectly. There was a wall of keys, each matched to one of thirty three vehicles of varying shapes, sizes and ages. One hook was missing its bounty, and a large empty space was in front of the enormous barn-style doors of the garage.

'Did they ram or push those doors open?' Furii asked the butler. 'There doesn't seem to be much damage.' He looked like she had just asked the most idiotic question ever.

'No madam, it is an automatic door. There is a remote installed in each vehicle.' He responded in his condescending way. Furii smirked. Of course they had a far better set up than she could even imagine.

'So they knew to use it. They also somehow got the vehicle out of those enormous front gates. Another remote? How did the guards not notice something was up?' These were direct questions lanced at the butler, rather than idle musings.

'Well, that is one of the issues. One of the main gate guards disappeared on the same night. Here and next door.'

'So, they was either involved, abducted or killed. It was at night? Surely vampires had to be involved. Does your boss have any main enemies who would want to sabotage her?'

'What lady of power does not? She can be acerbic at times, and many seek her hand in a union, but all are rejected.'

'So she may have a spurned lover... one that would steal her favourite human. Is she intimate with her human? What is his name for that matter?'

'That is hardly an appropriate question for me to answer. But jealousies may come into play in these situations. Over real or imagined events. His name was Gamboori Strength-in-his-Arms.'

'One of the native tribes.' Furii was surprised that someone so clearly racist would have a native man as her favourite feeder. 'At least I now may know a way to find him. Which vehicle was taken?'

'One of the largest her Grace owns, a saloon-style hearse, with space for two... well, it's passée, but coffins. It is an antique and can only be driven by humans during the day. It was made before our current driving technologies existed. Thus, it is highly valuable.' He explained with more reverence given than any other object mentioned. Furii was confused about the emphasis the Duchess placed on the single human rather than the other valuable items stolen. It was also notable that, amongst all the luxury vehicles present that they could have taken, they chose a cumbersome antique. Furii deduced that something must have happened that they needed to move some extra vampires than they had planned on. 'ampires stealing humans was not unheard of, but there were much easier marks than the highest levels of nobility.

'So the Duchie mentioned an emerald necklace and bracelet stolen, did you notice anything else missing?' Furii was purposely disrespectful about the full title of the Duchess, but the butler didn't even have a hint of a reaction.

'Mmm yes. Cash cards were stolen that were usually used by the staff and kept in a small security box in the foyer. More jewellery that her Grace had left by the door. Another thing to note is that they took all of these keys, and threw them on the floor under the cars. This was done so we could not give chase. Finding them all and sorting them was quite a task.' He implied that the task had fallen to him. Clearly he was put out by this whole event.

'Was there any staff with missing possessions?'

'No, thankfully.'

'Hmph. A considerate thief. Unusual,' she commented. The butler simply nodded. 'Was there anyone else on shift with the missing gate guard? Did anyone see what happened or were told anything?'

'No. The man rostered on with the guard was given leave to roam as we had issues with people attempting to enter the property via the side fences to use the pool or integrate into the parties her Grace hosts. So many of our guards check such areas periodically. It was during that half an hour used to do a circuit of the grounds that they absconded,' the butler explained. Furii nodded, noting how well planned this all was.

'Is there anything else to see? Any information regarding the direction they went?'

'No. They simply left after taking the car, and none saw a direction. You may wish to speak to the guards at the neighbouring estates, but my lady has not done so. So you will be taking the job?' he confirmed with Furii. She gave a sigh and nodded. It was hard enough to get work right now, and there was the none too subtle hint that she already knew too much to walk away safely. He tapped away on a comms pod that seemed to come from nowhere.

'Excellent. I have authorised a transfer of 10,000 bits as a down payment for your work and your discretion. I hope the Hellstorm clan were correct when they named you as their most deadly member. We believe this to be quite a large group who are committing these thefts, so take plenty of extra weaponry. Let none have a chance.'

'I... well, thank you. I am honoured they said that. I will do my... best?' Furii spoke with a questioning air, unsure as to whether it would be appropriate to promise to do her best at killing things. He seemed satisfied, however, and brusquely herded her out of the building. A foggy kind of morning was beginning to set in, and that was Furii's hint to start wrapping it up. She said her goodbyes and jumped back into her truck.

One last look at the mansion revealed that she was being intensely watched from the window by the mistress of the house. She didn't even flinch away when Furii stared back. This was turning out to be a bizarre case, not the least of which included the exorbitant amount they had volunteered to pay her. It was far above and beyond the Hellstorm clan's usual retainer fee. Furii had an uneasy feeling about all of this.

She was running against the sun to finish up the night, so Furii had to decide which of the neighbour's guards to interview. She opted for the most logical route- the neighbour one had to pass to get out of the city. Unfortunately, her luck failed, and the guards who were usually on that night were off. Furii left her contact details for them and drove home just as the sun was breaking the horizon.

Isabel was still in the exact same position, almost finished with the book she had started when Furii left. Even when Furii had dumped down her bag and comms pod, Isabel did not look up.

'Did you even move?' Furii asked sarcastically. Isabel blinked slowly and responded without moving.

'Move?'

'Yes, moved at all in the 3 hours I have been gone.'

'3 hours gone? No. What?' Isabel was still yet to tear her eyes away from her book while responding. Furii rolled her eyes and walked away without responding. At least she had taken the blood caps Furii had left out for her. If she wanted to spend her valuable sleeping time reading, that was her prerogative, especially as it kept the sassy little autophage quiet.

As she drifted off to sleep, Furii pondered her options. With 12,000 bits currently sitting in her bank account, it was an odd situation. As a last effort, she managed to order a new blood delivery before drifting off.

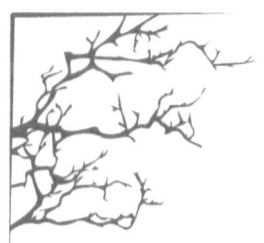

Chapter 6

'Well, what are you going to do?' Isabel asked Furii bluntly. She had been fast asleep on the couch, a book propped up on her chest, when Furii had first surfaced for the night. By the time Furii had showered Isabel was up and staring around with those odd dusty eyes. In no time she had started questioning the bounty hunter about her meeting.

'So, I haven't heard back from the guards, however I doubt they will have too much to contribute. But the missing man, Gamboori, is one of the Native people. The tribes people have ways of finding each other over long distances, something like a universal consciousness or divination. I learnt about their ways and lived amongst them for a while. If I contact them, I am sure Nakhari will help.' Furii was keen to see her friends again, especially as they were keen to repay her for lives saved.

'Nakhari?' asked Isabel, that spark of curiousity running through her demeanour again.

'Nakhari Weight-of-the-World. She is the seer of a tribe about 220 miles East. I found some of their children abducted by slave traders in the wastes one day. They led me back to the tribe, where it was explained that many of their human children get abducted in order to be sold to vampire nobility. In fact, I would not be entirely surprised if that is how Gamboori came to be in the employ of the Duchess in the first place.'

Isabel clicked her tongue. Her disapproval was plain to see, even with those dead grey eyes.

'The vampires of this city are really quite unpleasant,' she said earnestly, again reminding Furii that she was much older than she seemed. Furii couldn't help but laugh. Isabel looked peeved, but held her tongue for once.

'They certainly are. The nobility have always been bad, but last night truly showed how heinous they are. Regardless, the money they are paying me for this little gallivant is a fortune to me, and she wants it done as fast and as bloody as possible,' Furii explained, a pang of guilt crossing her mind when she spoke of gory work. Isabel had the grace to not mention it, which surprised Furii immensely. The autophage so loved needling her.

'So you will be driving to this place tonight then? Isn't the trip going to take longer than the night we have left? What about me?' Isabel asked, eyeing off the books again.

'Well I can't leave you here. It wouldn't be safe for you or the city. I don't trust the sheriff not to search the place while I am gone, nor you to stay where I put you. Even with books,' Furii added for good measure. Isabel looked saddened, and her entire posture slumped. Her tiny pointed shoulders jutted out of the t-shirt Furii had loaned her, ordinarily worn by a much more muscular woman.

'But I haven't finished reading all the books! Don't send me off to the wastes without them!' she begged desperately.

'You can take a book with you. I want to talk to the tribes to see if they know anything about sentient autophages anyway. They may be able to help, or hide, you.' Furii was immensely relieved when Isabel ceased her pleading.

'OK, one book. Will they search your death wagon on the way out? You are out of dead bodies to conceal me in.' There it was, Isabel was back to form. Furii groaned loudly.

'No, they tend not to, but I will find a way to hide you again. I need to get more ammunition and weapons, so go choose your book and get ready,' Furii chided as she grabbed her blood caps and keys. She passed some blood to Isabel and walked to the garage beneath her villa.

Her fresh blood delivery had been placed in a small two-way refrigerator by the door. The prompt delivery was a joy, as she would need these supplies for the trip. In reality, Furii had no idea how long it would take to both get to the tribe safely and convince them of the importance of aiding a city noble. Even with debts owed to Furii, it was a hard push to convince such an oppressed people to help their tormentors. Especially ones such as the Duchess Du Mort.

Still, there was ammunition to be purchasing. Furii stashed the blood into her on-board refrigerator and started the truck. Her garage door opened slowly, and Furii half expected to see the sheriff out front, surrounded by his goons. There were only the other quiet villas wedged together in her complex, bearing down upon her with their grey dereliction. Sometimes it was hard to believe that not only did people live there, but they also paid for the privilege.

Furii took the time to drive the extra distance to patron the armourer on Hellstorm grounds. That staff discount went a long way when you were paying by the bullet. Luckily there were few members of the clan around tonight, and those who were still in house were barely acquaintances to Furii. A casual nod to each and Furii could dart through the parking lot and gardens.

The Hellstorm compound was minuscule compared to the Du Mort estate, but it was functional. What was termed "gardens" were simply a series of outdoor training arenas, wrestling rings and even a gauntlet. The series of low warehouses nestled within the gardens were the complex proper. They contained lecture halls, more training grounds and the barracks to house all the interns and those in need of a place to crash. The armoury was safely stashed in the centre of the complex. This allowed it to both be well-guarded and on hand for anyone in desperate need of many ways to kill a critter.

Her luck holding, Furii made it to the door of the weapons trader without having to spend any time trapped in small talk. At the door she came face to face with Nathan Hellstorm, however. This was a tad awkward, because last time they were face to face, she had threatened to castrate him with her scythes. Furii had even pressed them against his manhood, stepping close to watch the sweat beading on his brow. Not that he had much to remove, however. She knew that from personal experience when he had exposed himself to her.

This time he looked like a kicked puppy, wincing away from Furii and instinctively holding his crotch. Nathan scuttled away as fast as his short legs could take him. Furii smirked happily, hoping that no other young intern would have to suffer with seeing his dehydrated shrimp.

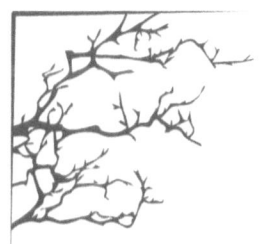

Chapter 7

The Hellstorm armoury was enormous, with row upon row of weapons. There was almost anything you could imagine to maim, kill or heal if needed. Furii grabbed some spare knives before heading over to get some bullets and extra crossbow bolts. As always, Vincenza was manning the high counter protected by Plexiglas and her own lethal skills. Vincenza was tall, broad-shouldered and had enormous breasts that spilled from every shirt she wore. Even though she was stuck in the body of someone in their late 40s, she was a highly desirable force to be reckoned with. Luckily, most of the boys like Nathan were utterly terrified of her. There was a lot that Furii admired about Vincenza.

'Hunter 4095, how goes the hunt?' she asked as she threw aside her usual reading material, a pulpy fiction novel.

'Not too bad, Vinnie. I am going to need a heck of a stock up for my next one,' Furii responded, her fondness for Vincenza leaking honey tones into her voice. The armourer looked surprised.

'You? Needing more than just running in headfirst with a sickle in each hand? Catching fangs with that bougie armour you have?' She was suitably sarcastic. More to like.

'Well apparently it is potentially a whole score of kidnapping bandits, who the Duchess wants annihilated.'

'Duchess? Which one?' Vincenza asked drily as she began to put on her safety gear for dispensing palo santo crossbow bolts.

'Du Mort.' Furii kept it blunt and simple. Vincenza physically cringed.

'Rest in peace. Here lies Hunter 4095, Furii of the Hellstorm clan.'

'Thanks. That bad?' Furii clarified, feeling like she may have underestimated how much trouble she was in this time.

'Well, did you go to her mansion?'

'Yes.'

'Did you see all the windows?'

'Yes.'

'Many of those are rooms specifically created to Greet the Sun. The Du Mort family finds a perverted joy in watching those who have failed them crispify over long minutes in the morning sun. They boast about a 17-minute record breaker, a beefy fellow who took that long to fry. I mean, they earned their name from their cruelty and their volatility. Even the hunting clans have no power over them when they decide to nuke a member who hasn't lived up to their expectations of a hunt well done,' Vincenza explained without a hint of over-embellishment. Furii just nodded slowly.

'In that case, throw in some explosives,' she said flatly. Vincenza smiled, bringing out those gorgeous dimples she knew brought grown adults to their knees. She quickly packed up the crossbow bolts, spare wood for stakes, Furii's preferred bullets and a small collection of explosives. As she went to pay Furii decided to throw in a first aid kit in case the human was damaged. While collecting up the goods she had brought, Furii noticed some unusual sleek little pods in with the explosives. She picked one up and raised an eyebrow at Vincenza.

'That is one of mine. They can be scooted quietly across soft surfaces, slid on hard surfaces, skipped like a stone across water, and if you pull the two halves apart it reveals a sticky core that can be attached to most surfaces. They can be set to a timer or remotely activated via your comms pod. Just have to sync them up to it. Gives a heck of a bang thanks to a new explosive compound I perfected. Make sure you are at least 50 feet away when you detonate it. Even then you might get a mighty good tan.' Vincenza was clearly so proud of her remarkable creation. Furii turned the slate grey pod back and forth in her hands, feeling the seam down the middle where it was supposed to split in half. She tested it gently, admiring the way it slid open. The sticky core was exactly as described, with a firm adhesive stretching between the two halves.

'It's a wonder, Vincenza. Beautiful design. I will make sure they are thoroughly tested!' Furii said joyfully.

'I tell you this every time kiddo, Vinnie.' She chided the younger vampire.

'I wasn't raised like that.' Furii argued gently, hard to break out of the early days in the clan, with protocol for the older vampires beaten into her.

'We are Hellstorm. We were raised exactly the same you, doofus.' Vincenza smiled as she entered the purchase amount into her payment system and Furii paid with her comms pod.

Thankfully she had been paid so much more for the secrecy around contaminated autophages, as this had not been a cheap shopping trip. She hefted her bags over her shoulder and said her goodbyes. Vincenza smiled after her, relishing a proud sense of admiration for her clan sister. Especially after she heard the tale about the run-in between Furii and Nathan.

Rather than seek the glory and death of trawling the wastes, Vincenza had accepted the role of armourer in favour of peaceful nights. She by far preferred to tinker with highly dangerous gadgets. The rest of the Hellstorm clan greatly appreciated the fruits of her labour, which often gave them the edge over the other clans,

When all of her new goods were safely packed into her truck, Furii headed home. She was furiously workshopping ideas of how to sneak Isabel out of the city. So much so that she took no notice of the trip home, nor her usual checks to see if she was being followed. As Furii reversed into her garage, she mentally kicked herself for being so distracted.

Isabel sat on the couch, three books piled by her side. She had at least showered. Furii was curious to note that her skin seemed less grey, her fingers less pointed. Her eyes still brought typhoons to mind.

'Isabel, I said ONE book, not three.' She felt like she was nagging at this point.

'No but I need both of these as they are a trilogy for this one, and I have already read half of it. I have to know what happens,' the younger 'phage argued back. Furii sighed. It was not worth the breath to argue.

'Fine. Now we need to figure out how to smuggle you out of here. Let's go look at the truck.'

They circled the truck, looking for any way to conceal Isabel safely. There were a few little spaces that would have worked well, but were difficult to access. Some were far too easy to see. By far the best space was towards the front of the rear cabin, where there was a large body-sized gap beneath the floor. Unfortunately, it was incredibly hard to access without removing parts of the vehicle. Furii sighed all of her frustration out in one scorching exhalation. Isabel simply stood there, her lips in a moue of defeated deep thought. Looking around the garage, her face brightened.

'I can fit in this!' she said excitedly, dragging out a compact suitcase. Furii looked doubtful. Isabel's eyes darted between Furii and the case, back and forth, assessing her reaction. Finally she just threw it open and climbed in.

'Ta-dah! It's a perfect fit. We can do this!'

In response Furii simply groaned, conceding to the overly excited autophage. Let the kid volunteer for being completely uncomfortable and crammed into a suitcase. Furii was sure that if she suggested it, Isabel would have been furious. She walked back into the apartment to collect spare clothing and toiletries enough to last a few days on the road. There was no way to tell how long it would take to figure out where the tribe was on their lands, let alone discuss all she needed to. Begging the shaman to look for Gamboori was hard enough, but the ritual required to locate him was of uncertain length. It could take days to find his trail. Luckily, being a human meant that he was too valuable to kill, so short of a misadventure, he should remain alive.

With her essentials packed, Furii returned to the garage after securing her house. Isabel had already grabbed her books and was waiting with the suitcase. They lifted the suitcase into the back first before Isabel got in, making it easier on Furii. When she was safely zipped up and stashed behind a few other bags of supplies, it occurred to Furii that it was inherently lucky that vampires, and by extension autophages, didn't need to breathe. Despite being a battered old case, it was still quite airtight.

She jumped into the cab and opened the garage door. Its creaking rumble felt soothingly normal in a decidedly abnormal day.

It's just another hunt. It's just another hunt. Furii repeated to herself, trying to soothe away the intuition that it was anything but.

Furii gulped with nerves as she reached the gate out of the city. She had to battle to keep her thoughts neutral and not show any physical signs of her fear. As she drove up to the checkpoint, an apathetic guard barely glanced up before waving her through.

That was it.

After all that tension, she had been dismissed from suspicion with a wave from a man who may as well have been swatting at a fly. Furii almost felt cheated, but she wasn't about to tempt fate. A few miles out from the city, she stopped and let Isabel out. The autophage happily sat in the passenger seat without a single snarky comment. As she turned the pages of her book, Furii was surprised to notice that her hands had less of a dark grey hue. That spider-like quality that autophages had was slowly going. Some flesh had smoothed out the lumps of her knuckles and the fingers themselves were a lot less pointed. She even had new hair sprouting where the thin, stringy mess had been.

'Isabel, show me your eyes,' Furii asked gently.

'Hmm?' Isabel queried she looked up. They were the same storm-soaked grey, without a hint of red.

'Never mind,' responded Furii, focusing on the journey ahead. They had a lot of ground to cover.

When the dawn was just preparing to break, Furii shut down the truck. She activated the daytime shields and climbed into the back of the truck via an internal door. She gestured for Isabel to do the same. Handing Isabel a worn bed roll, Furii felt apologetic.

'Sorry it is my old one, but it is all I had.'

''That's fine, I used to sleep on the floor back at the... well... hole I lived in before. Sleeping on the couch has been practically a luxury,' she quipped. Again, Furii was surprised at the magnanimity of this odd little autophage. She dosed out some blood caps for each of them from her fridge and they soon settled in to sleep the day away. The truck was both armoured against attack and shielded fully from the sun, so they had very little to worry about.

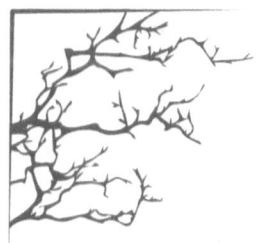

Chapter 8

Furii automatically woke as the sun set, stretching quietly to avoid waking Isabel. She climbed into the cab with all the stealth she could muster and tapped open her comms pod. There was little of interest around; one or two inconsequential bounties had been posted, nothing like the job she was on now. Furii didn't have friends to send her messages, so it was all work. She jumped as the thing began to ring in her hand. It was an unknown number, but she answered it anyway.

'Furii Hellstorm? This is guard 59 at the Earl Wintergrim estate. You requested I call,' came a severe voice, with no time for softness.

'Yes, I believe you were one of the guards on duty when the Du Mort estate was attacked?'

'Yes, and now I am the only guard who was on the gate. Guard 45 has since gone missing.' He sounded even more cagey about the subject, if that was possible.

'You mean after the attack, a guard at the next estate went missing too?' Furii clarified, feeling like this was rapidly spiralling into something far greater.

'Yes, it was reported immediately after she did not check in for the debrief. No one has had contact since.'

'So I should also look for a female guard in a Wintergrim uniform. Did you see anything yourself that night?' Furii queried, knowing that it would probably be a useless endeavour.

'No. Guard 45 did a road patrol, I know she goes and gossips to her friend at the Du Mort estate when she does. It has never been an issue before. Then I... lost focus. For a short while. One of the inner compound guards er... alerted... my focus... when they came to cover my break. By the reports, it was over by then,' he said in an almost whisper. Clearly, he did not want his colleagues to know that he had fallen asleep on the job, while his fellow guard was off being abducted or murdered. Furii shook her head. She signed off curtly, rather disgusted by the guard, and sat back in her seat.

Closing down the pod, Furii tapped impatiently on the steering wheel as she waited for Isabel to wake. Cacophonous snores started up from the kid as she rolled onto her back. Figuring that the engine would be much quieter than that racket, Furii turned over the engine and slowly raised the shields. The night had fallen enough that the sun was simply tendrils of light, piercing the few clouds around the horizon.

Isabel continued to snore, which amused Furii no end, because vampires did not need to breathe. Perhaps it was a residual habit of her previous life as a human, or a connection to her animalistic autophage nature. Whatever the cause, Furii found it profoundly entertaining.

The miles rolled on and eventually Isabel surfaced, stretching out stiff limbs. She sat in silence as she acclimatised to consciousness again. After almost an hour had passed, she finally spoke.

'How far away do you think we are?' She tried to not make it sound whiny or bored at least.

'At least three hours. The noble families of the city ensured there was no way for the Natives to easily return when they assigned the reservations. They kept a thoroughly uncomfortable amount of space between the two locations entirely on purpose,' Furii explained as Isabel snorted derisively.

'So the bluebloods like the native people about as well as my people. What a surprise.' The sarcasm that coated every word lanced hard through the air. Furii nodded grimly. It was hard to disagree with the truth.

'The only time they like the tribes-people is when they are doing their menial tasks. They have been secretly trading the humans of the tribes still, if Gamboori is anything to go by. I find it ironic that the Duchess was willing to take him as a lover, however. That part is a shock. The modern-day slavery is less so.'

'So, you knew about the slavery and trade of humans?' Isabel asked with a note of judgement woven into her words.

'I had suspicions, but prior to last night, I had no proof. I had never been to any of the noble estates before, let alone talked to any of the staff. Until now I only met nobles at the Hellstorm compound. All I know is rumours and gossip.' Furii pursed her lips after she finished speaking. Luckily, Isabel took the hint and stopped asking about a subject Furii clearly took deeply personally. It may have been many centuries since her people were enslaved, but the generational wound still stung.

'So, these people are shitty, but we are still doing this weird mission for a ridiculous amount of money because we are broke, right?' Isabel asked without venom in her harsh words. She flexed those still mostly spider-like hands as she spoke, reminiscent of those spindly arachnids that once haunted the cornices of every home. As with everything else, they were now extinct.

'That, and we either do this awful mission, or I die horribly. The Duchess made that part clear. She likes to watch people fry in the sun while timing it for kicks. An all-round charming woman, you see?' Furii felt bitter and sarcastic, and it tainted her every word. Isabel eeped quietly.

'Let's not let that happen then. Not a good option.' She muttered as she opened her book and buried herself in it. Furii drove on, the expanse of the dusty wasteland drying her soul.

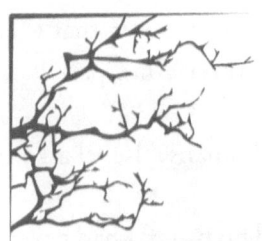

Chapter 9

Nothing changed out here. The rusty rocks were ground into sand by the wind, the sand into dust. Death and desolation were absolute. When the vampire spread had killed the biodiversity, the land soon followed. Trees were obsolete aside from those tended to in the city. Animals were long gone, any remnants devoured by roaming autophages. All that was left was bitter dust. This far out from any shelter the winds buffeted her truck, sand blasting its already speckled paintwork.

Furii was beginning to cramp up in her calves and feet when the Native reserve appeared on the horizon. There was no high rise here, no spires to insult the sky. The lights were all low to the ground, a warmer, more welcoming glow than the city could ever offer. Furii stopped the truck a few miles out again to re-conceal Isabel. Once satisfied she was hidden, Furii drove to the main entrance. A smiling guard stopped her to check the newcomer in, as was standard practice on the reserves.

'Bounty hunter 4095, Furii Hellstorm. I am here to consult with Nakhari Weight-of-the-World about a case,' Furii explained as she showed her identity card.

'Nakhari told us you would be coming, along with your friend. You are both welcome to enter and go to the Seer Home. Have you been before?' the guard asked, still smiling away, their dimples showing in a most adorable manner. Furii was too speechless at the comment clearly directed at Isabel. Nakhari knew that Furii was bringing an autophage into her town and yet had apparently approved her entry? She was stunned. Furii knew the seer was good, but had no idea she was this good.

'But Isabel... autophage... she is welcome?' Furii asked incredulously. The guard simply smiled up at her even brighter. They had long straight hair, braided and looped either side of their face. Furii found them to be utterly charismatic, and slowly relaxed the tension in her limbs. Their indeterminate gender was entirely normal amongst the native tribes, another detail Furii remembered from the first time she had dealt with Nakhari. 'You mean to say you know I have an autophage hidden away and you approve of it?'

'Yes. Nakhari said you had the best of intentions and require aid in protecting the autophage. Those were her exact words, I believe. So please, go to Seer Home and seek her there. She will help you for both of your current challenges.' The smiling guard waved her through. Furii was starting to remember how unnerving it had been amongst these people, their intensely intuitive nature and ability to truth seek. She both loved and hated it.

When she was safely parked outside Seer House, Furii let Isabel out of the bag.

'So I guess I am to hide in here until you are done? Good, I am up to a good part of my book. You see, there is this faery girl and she is...' Isabel fell silent as Furii shook her head.

'No, Nakhari knows you are here. She will want to meet you.'

'Why does she know I am here? How? Why are they fine with me being here? I would rather read my book.' Isabel sulked quietly.

'These people are gifted with prophesies and truth-seeking. Nakhari is their shaman, and most powerful. She somehow knew about you, and that you are an autophage. But we are keeping her waiting right now, which could be seen as disrespectful, so...' Furii hinted in her usual manner- lacking all common subtlety. Isabel grumped and groaned as she packed her books away. She was extremely reticent to leave the safety of seclusion. Furii jerked her head, indicating that it was time to move out. While Isabel may have felt unsafe, Furii knew that the tribe had to follow the word of Nakhari. The shaman allowing

Isabel to enter the town alone meant that she would be safe. That was still hard to tell someone who had been hunted for a great deal of time and had witnessed the killing of her family. Furii was guiltily curious at that thought.

'How can you tolerate still being around when I killed your family? I thought you would have run off by now. Surely you can't just be staying for the books?' she asked Isabel as they approached the door to the Seer Home. Isabel stopped to think a moment.

'The books are a big draw, and I have contemplated it. But my family... they were already gone. I knew what they were, I had seen them do horrific things. But they were all I had, so I stayed there. I couldn't kill them myself, and they offered some sort of protection. I hate how it happened, but I know this is a chance at a new path.' As Isabel spoke, Furii was struck at how mature she sounded. Despite the physical changes that revealed Isabel to be an autophage, she was clearly wise and filled with intelligence. Furii felt reassured that saving Isabel was the best decision, despite the sheriff and his attitude.

'Aye, that is a good point. Did you get a chance to meet the Indigenous folks before everything happened?' she asked of the kid, realising she knew very little about her travelling companion.

'Not really. I had mostly heard stories about them or seen the occasional person in the city. They seem to know you though.' Isabel commented, referring to the many nods of greeting they received from passing folk. Furii smiled.

'I lived amongst these people for a while, and honestly I would have stayed if it were at all possible. Nakhari is a lifelong sister to me, and happens to be the shaman here. She is the reason I am accepted by these people. I may have saved a group of their children, but as a bounty hunter, I was mistrusted by the tribe. They thought that I may be attempting to get access to the tribe to take more people to enslave. But Nakhari was the only one who saw the truth about me, in my heart. She allowed me to stay and healed my wounds. She taught me their culture and mythology. Did you know that their people had long prophesied the vampire plague?" As she finished speaking, a face appeared in the doorway.

Oh, we have kept them waiting too long!' exclaimed Furii. She bowed and trotted over, Isabel following behind begrudgingly.

'Sorry, I was just explaining to Isabel about the culture here. She has never been in the tribe lands before.' The seer apprentice nodded, designated by their simple headdress.

Bones were interwoven with hair and flat pieces of metal to create a winged style decoration. Their eyes were the pale green of the newest shoots of desert grasses, their skin the colour of the smoke-clad sun. They were very gender ambiguous, and Furii knew them to be a mediator, someone between a man and a woman. Many seer folk were outside the gender binary forced upon those in the city, but were considered entirely normal.

'Avari, bring them here. I wish to see my sister who stinks of death as always.' A growling shout rang through the hallways, filled with a sense of jovial familiarity.

'Yea Seer-Sister.' Avari responded with a voice fettered by timidity. The junior seer beckoned for them to follow.

The hall was rather long, with rooms branching off regularly along its mighty path. The inside of this house was deceptively large. Isabel caught glimpses of prone bodies and bloodied wounds, while Furii stared directly ahead. There was a door at the end painted black, with stars and constellations embellished upon it. This was where the voice had come from, where the healer tending to all the people in the previous rooms retired to. Furii felt a surge of anticipation and nerves. As Avari raised their hand to knock, the door was thrown open. There stood Nakhari, with a large bone headdress spearing the air, chains of tiny bones framing her face in sharded waterfalls. Her face was that of someone well into her 50's, with laugh lines aplenty. The seer was so tall that even the intimidating Furii looked short. Nakhari wore clothes that were intricately embroidered, little frozen scenes of the mythological history of her people. Threaded gods and monsters fought between vibrant creation myths, all alive in rich colour and delicate stitches. Her long grey hair fell in wispy masses to her waist, filled with braids and small beads. That unusual growling voice came from this indomitable woman.

'Furii, my sister of blood and grist, you are late.' She chided, a deep growl rolling beneath her words.

'I had to stop multiple times for Isabel. How did you know she was coming, and why have you allowed any autophage to enter the reserve, let alone the seer house?' Furii asked bluntly. Nakhari giggled, although it was more a low, rough bark of mirth.

'Ever the sword, Furii, cutting to the core of the topic. I knew because the wind whispered of your approach with one of the corrupted. The land spoke of her footfalls, with thought and presence. The ether roared with her tainted energy and acute intellect. We know of the new autophages, but those in the city conceal their existence. Bomehari, come here.' Nakhari called out.

After some awkward shuffling in a room over, an older vampire came out; however, her hair and eyes were both pure grey. Her fingers were long, but not as viciously pointed as an autophage's, and her skin was the normal pale of the vampire. Bomehari was wearing the robes of a seer initiate, with the simpler bone headdress Avari wore. The prefix of -ari was added to the names of all shamans, seer and initiate alike. Bomehari viewed Isabel with fascinated caution.

'Yes, Nakhari?' she asked politely, but clearly knew full well why she was summoned.

'Bomehari is an autophage that retained her faculties and, once fed adequately, almost entirely reverted to a usual vampire form. I am sure you have noticed changes in Isabel too,' Nakhari explained freely. Furii was so acclimatised to false niceties used to conceal subterfuge that she felt delighted to be with the pragmatic seer once again. Isabel looked surprised.

'Yes, I have seen some changes in Isabel, even though it's only been days. How is that possible?' Furii asked.

'They are still vampires; they still have their ability to heal rapidly. The ones who retain their mind, anyway. The others seem unable to ever return, sadly.' As Nakhari spoke, Isabel began to tear up.

'You mean I could be normal again?' she pleaded with Nakhari.

'Yes, but your eyes and hair will never revert to normal colour. They will always be grey. But most of the other changes will revert.' Furii felt a burst of joy woven with guilt in her heart as Nakhari spoke.

'The sheriff wants all autophages dead. He knows about the sentient ones and paid me a lot of money to kill Isabel too. Maybe he doesn't know they can heal? He was pretty adamant about keeping the public afraid of autophages.' A thoughtful look crossed Furii's face as she spoke, intent on the malicious machinations of the city vampires.

'You know why they do it, Furii. Those in the city require these artificial situations to maintain their control. Now, the second reason you are here.' Nakhari nodded to Bomehari, who disappeared into another room. She then gestured to a low table with pillows rather than chairs around it. A fur lay upon it, and over that a map was spread out. Isabel and Furii sat down carefully, trying to perch themselves comfortably on the odd little hard cushions favoured by Nakhari. Furii spoke first.

'I have to find a missing man, Gamboori. He was a human servant in the Du Mort family. Being of the tribes, I was hoping you could find him,' Furii explained, her eyes bright and demeanour relaxed in the presence of her old friend. Nakhari snorted loudly, making the bones in her hair clack in chorus.

'The Du Morts? They didn't just use the satellite tracker?'

'No? What do you mean? He would have to be tagged for a tracker to work.' Furii asked, confusion creasing the wrinkles on her forehead.

'Yeah, exactly. The über-rich families such as the Du Morts implant trackers onto all of their feeding stock. Especially our kind, having a tendency to abscond after being abducted and all that. The families track them back to the tribes and get the sheriffs to raid us. It's the only possible way they could have known.' As she spoke, Nakhari's face flushed with anger. It was only when she swallowed hard that Isabel noticed the presence of a small Adam's apple. She stayed silent, preferring to ask Furii about it later.

'They didn't mention any of that at all. The butler showed me around but wouldn't even let me into the house they kept the humans in, nor could I talk to them. The people who took Gamboori also took a very specific car, and some valuables. I was mostly hoping that he had just escaped and taken the car with him.'

'Why is that not possible now?' Isabel interjected curiously. Nakhari answered this time.

'Because otherwise he would be here. And we would have been raided the night after. The fact that we haven't indicates that they also know where he is.' As Nakhari spoke, Furii swore under her breath.

'So why the hell do they have me looking for him? And why did I have to try and track him myself? What the hell are they playing at?' Furii sat dejected, running flustered fingers through her dreadlocks. The light in her eyes had dulled, a deep burgundy leaking through her pupils. Anger simmered through the air, cloying and choking. It wound around the trio like an irate cat marking its territory. The sensation of being strangled, drowning in a viscous mess grew as Isabel started to panic.

'Furii, stop,' Nakhari said firmly. The feeling vanished as soon as Furii came to, sitting up straighter and blinking. The darkness slowly left her pupils, returning to their usual pale red. Isabel slumped down in relief at being released from that emotional miasma. 'Now to answer your questions, I don't know. But I can find where he is if you can control your aura. I didn't teach you our ways so you could waste them on temper tantrums!'

'I'm sorry. I haven't been practising, and I was so caught up. The lies and the manipulations they orchestrate in the noble classes are infuriating. Like, why me? I don't deal with nobles.' Furii still sounded a little petulant, but Nakhari just laughed.

'Let's get this search done so you stop aggrieving me over this.' As she spoke, Nakhari drew a handful of tiny bones and rocks out of her pocket. 'I don't often get a chance to use the tiny ones!' she said gleefully.

With a whispered word to the clutched bones, Nakhari cast them onto the map. They fell across it in a jumble, the stones bouncing into their positions and the bones clanking against each other as they found their space. Nakhari stared down at them before picking them up one by one and meditating with each.

'A trap here. An ambush, bandits. Don't stop here. Here there will be water, but I suppose that is not useful for either of you. Here there will be a death. Here, this is where Gamboori is.' She finally pointed to a position on the map. Furii copied each point down in her comms pod carefully. Furii was astounded, expecting there to be a far longer, more meditational ritual to find him. This was almost easy.

'Thank you Nakhari. Is there anything else you are picking up about the place?' Furii's question was reverent, solemn in its delivery. Isabel was amused by how seriously Furii was taking this. In her mind, a few rocks and half a dead lizard did not give this kind of information.

'The place he is held is underground. The entrance is deceptively lightly guarded. There are many lies woven around every part of this; before this is over, you will be betrayed. Illusions rise and fall. The blood is the path and the binding.' Nakhari's eyes were unfocused and eerily large when she slowly turned her head towards Isabel. 'This one shall be the canary in the mine. You must take this one to the source. Her ties are those who will unbind your fetters, Furii Hellstorm.' Isabel shivered. There was something about that deep gaze and talk of her own past that dug deep into her core and made her a believer. Isabel could feel so much more going on now than just some stones on a map.

They almost seemed performative and incidental compared to what the seer was now doing.

Prickles of sensation tickled over her dusky skin.

She swallowed hard.

A background buzz became audible.

The feeling of being watched by multitudinous eyes smothered Isabel. She felt as though the room was suddenly too crowded. They studied her intensely, picking over every flaw, every concealed secret. Invisible hands tugged at her hair and sent goosebumps skittering across her skin.

Isabel averted her eyes.

The clamp of the seer's attention laxed. It withdrew back into Nakhari as her eyes focused on the physical world again. She blinked slowly to relieve the dehydration of not blinking for such a long period. Isabel was now quaking slightly, but Furii seemed not to notice.

'What do you mean I have to take her? I only brought her out here to set her loose. I thought your people may have a solution or some little bolt hole for her to live. I cannot do this task with a little tag along. I work alone. Goddamnit, NO!' Furii became more irate as Nakhari sat there silently and serenely. This served to only make Furii even angrier. She glared and huffed until she finally just stood and stormed out. Nakhari looked at Isabel almost apologetically.

'Don't worry about it, dear. She gets in these moods at times. The whole Hellstorm clan are the same, really.' She offered. Isabel just flexed her spider-like hands distractedly, worrying at the dark grey tip of each finger. She nodded quietly. The sprouted wisps of her hair shifted gently in the breeze generated by Furii throwing open the tent flap at the end of the hall.

'Can... can I ask a question?' Isabel asked quietly. The red eyes of the shaman turned back to fix themselves on the now-squirming autophage.

'Is it about you healing or the fact that I was born a man?' Nakhari asked bluntly. Isabel shivered in shock.

'N- no, I wanted to know... why I was like this, but my family wasn't. They were gone mentally. It wasn't about the... oh dear.' Isabel felt the fire of an intense blush flood her body. While vampires no longer had the blood flow to properly blush, they still felt the shivers of heat and pins.

'Yes 'It's OK kiddo" as my sister Furii would say' Nakhari teased gently.

'Hey, I was 19 when I caught vampirism and that was 120 years ago!' Isabel sulked, the result coming off even more endearing. Nakhari laughed, a gravelly chortle that warmed the area.

'In tribal tradition we are open about gender. I was born as a male, but from the moment I could express myself, I wanted to be female. The tribe rallies around the child and has a rebirthing ceremony. They are then treated wholly as the other gender. These children are often sent to learn under the seer, as they have a sacred view of duality and can represent all people within the tribe when we speak to the spirits. Bomehari was born between male and female, and thus is even more sacred. This was why I could convince the tribe to accept an autophage within our walls. Since they have seen their good spirit, none contest their right to live amongst us.' Nakhari stopped a moment to rest her splintered voice. Isabel sat transfixed, silently waiting for her to begin speaking. There was something in the weary way Nakhari spoke that was riveting. The listener had a feeling that the literal weight of the world was on Nakhari's shoulders, and that her every beleaguered word was essential. Finally, she continued.

'Bomehari's tribal name is Bomehari Walks-Between-Worlds, and this is true for both gender and life. When I pass, they will be seer, and will herald a golden era for the tribe. They will propel them forward in unimaginable ways, if the city does not intervene. I see this, but the cloud of those buzzards in the city may subvert this destiny. Now, about the autophages. Simply put, I don't know why some change and some keep their wits. From meeting Bomehari and yourself, I can say that you are both destined for great things. Perhaps it is destiny that keeps you sane. Perhaps your sanity gives you a remarkable destiny. Either way, both of you will change this world immeasurably,' Nakhari finished up as Furii walked back into the room. She was exceedingly grouchy, but at least she had stopped shouting.

'Better hope it will be world-changing if I have to bring this kid along. Avari said it's time for the gathering.' Her mutter was barely audible even to sensitive vampire ears. A wrinkle of displeasure still marred her forehead, her shoulders slouched beneath her body armour. Nakhari ignored it completely and clapped her hands together happily.

'Come little autophage, time for you to spurn the dawn with us.' The seer stood and lightly stepped out, the folds of her robe trailing behind her retreating form. Isabel rushed to stand, almost toppling back over with the effort. Furii just grunted and walked out of the tent, with Isabel scampering behind her.

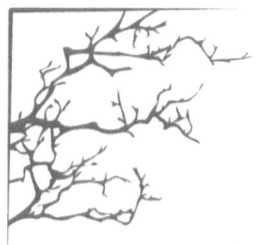

Chapter 10

The gathering occurred around the large fire in front of the seer's home. There was adequate space for the whole tribe to encircle the deep fire pit along with their guests. Isabel eagerly took the offered seat beside Nakhari, looking from person to person, taking in the vibrant colours of their beautiful clothes, adorned with various pieces of old and abandoned technological waste. There were no longer enough animals for furs, so the people of the wastes made clothing from any scrap they found. Wires were woven into fabrics, plastic covers were used for structural garments and scraps of old material were dyed with vivid colours to make up the more gentle components of their clothing. Headpieces with bones were popular, and many featured pieces of computer chips and scraps of coloured glass and metal that glinted in the firelight.

The gathered tribe listened to the seer reverently, and regarded the two newcomers curiously.

'Tribe-kin, tonight we announce the sad passing of one of our own, a human. Zossbel has left this plane due to ageing, and thus returns to the land. In remaining human, he chose a life that was fleeting but sacred. He gave us the gift of our sustenance and as such he served the tribe with great integrity.' Nakhari hesitated as several humans began to wail. The whole tribe waited for them to calm themselves, with vampires and humans alike giving way to sobbing. Eventually they calmed down again, gently soothed by their neighbours. Nakhari spoke again.

'We shall complete his funerary rites tomorrow night, after the family and his friends have had enough time to make their last goodbyes. Any who wish to do so shall contact the human family first. Now we have his final offering, his requested last gift to the tribe.' Nakhari held her arm out to two male vampires holding a great bowl between them. It was filled with blood, Zossbel's final gift. Small but ancient wooden cups were given to each of the tribe members who, in turn, took a cupful and drank deeply. Isabel joined in enthusiastically, but gave a quizzical look when Furii quietly walked away. She looked at Nakhari who inclined her head towards the back of the fierce bounty hunter.

'She never did drink like this. Never shared her reasons either, in all the time she lived amongst us. Always just swallowing those pills. We accept her, but those scars run deep.' Nakhari spoke as she took the last cup of liquid. The entire vampire line of the tribe had drunk their fill before Nakhari had hers; even the seer apprentices drank before her. Isabel was starting to understand the role of the seer, both a leader and caretaker.

'The pills aren't so bad. When you see your 'phage family tear into anything that moves... well... it starts to make sense,' explained Isabel. Nakhari smiled fondly at the little autophage who had finally started to crack the killer.

The assembled vampires mostly spoke amongst themselves for the rest of the gathering. Occasionally they would break out into song, or one would stand to share a story. Furii returned to the group once they had finished drinking but still stood on the outskirts with a scowl on her face. Nakhari sidled over to her as soon as the opportunity presented itself.

'Furii, you know that you already care for the child, why resist it?' She chided gently. Furii looked mulish.

'I don't need to be burdened with any creature right now. I don't need any attachment right now. Or ever. Leave her here, she has others here. I'm the one who killed her parents anyway.' Furii muttered as she watched the streamers made from strips of fabric flutter in the light. Deep shades of purple, orange and crimson adorned every roof, dangled from every pole and were worn by every member to designate the tribe. Her idle gaze was interrupted by Nakhari stepping right up into her face.

'Yet the omens and the spirits both say you must take her with you.'

'You know I don't believe in the spirits, Nakhari,' Furii snapped back, attracting glances from the members of the tribe closest to them.

'Regardless of your belief or not, they still speak the truth. Shall I tell you what they think of your attitude?' Nakhari retorted with a smile. Furii snorted in frustration but didn't respond. Nakhari continued. 'Excellent. We will start the modifications to your truck tomorrow, so you can smuggle her in and out of the city. Dinelae has been aching to work on your vehicle again.'

This made Furii finally snap to attention and look at Nakhari.

'If Dinelae knows about it and can start work tomorrow...' She stopped talking abruptly, knowing the response and realising she was totally outnumbered.

'Yes, she has already fabricated the capsule, it just needs to be attached. It can be done in a few hours of the day.' Nakhari explained, holding her hand out for the expected keys. Furii sighed loudly and handed them over. There was no fighting this. Nakhari shouted to Dinelae, who stood by the fire, loudly explaining something while gesturing wildly. The reed-thin woman trotted over, her red hair enhanced by the dancing flames all around. She grabbed the keys with a cheeky smile and took off to drive Furii's vehicle into her garage.

The glow of the sun beginning to rise was staining the horizon, signalling that the gathering was coming to an end. Tribe members kissed and hugged each other goodbye. They were all so happy, and amongst them Isabel was grinning widely. Each member of the tribe slowly returned to their homes, so Isabel trotted over to Furii and Nakhari.

'Are we sleeping in the truck again?' She asked.

'No, the truck has already been abducted by the madness of this tribe.' Furii was still a little grouchy.

'We have rooms prepared for you both in the Seer's house. They are safe and cool. The desert sun shall not mar your sleep. Avari will show you to the rooms while I finish the rituals of the moonset.' Nakhari shuffled off and indicated to Avari that they were ready. Bomehari joined Nakhari and they kneeled facing the direction where the moon was rapidly being devoured by the light of the rising dawn.

Furii was quick to fall in line behind Avari, keen to be back in seclusion. Isabel followed shortly after, taking a moment to watch the rituals of the two seers. They bent and flowed in the growing light, their arms reaching towards the horizon or up into the sky. It was a magical union between earth and being, a serenade to all that was natural.

Furii had her boots off and feet up in her modest little room when Isabel walked in dragging her blanket. Her eyes were huge, a sense of panic in their grey depths.

'What do you want, kid?' Furii asked tiredly, but without malice.

'I feel weird sleeping alone in this hut thing. Can I sleep in here with you? I will sleep on the floor. I just can't sleep.' Isabel asked quietly, shifting from side to side in embarrassment. Despite the 'kid' being hundreds of years old, Furii couldn't help but view Isabel as being so young. Then again, Furii had found immortality in her 30's. All teenagers, even those in the late teen years, seemed like babies then.

'Fine, you can have that half of the bed, just don't kick me. Keep on your side,' Furii muttered as she moved over and put her back to the room. Isabel thanked her profusely as she climbed into the bed. Soon they were both fast asleep as the sun crossed the sky.

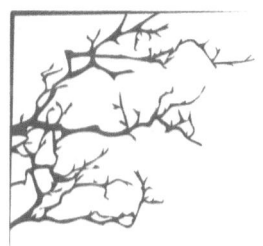

Chapter 11

When they woke, it was to the calls for the first meal of the day. Furii was alarmed to find Isabel curled up to her arm, wrapped around it as though the scarred limb was a teddy bear. She tried to extract herself stealthily, but ended up waking Isabel regardless. Those big doe eyes blinked slowly in the half light. Furii pulled the rest of the way out from under her blankets and stood up with a stretch punctuated by the creaks and pops of her joints. Isabel laughed as she sprang out of bed, full of vigour.

The advantage of being turned as a teen, Furii thought bitterly. Taking no notice of the glare from Furii, Isabel gathered little pieces of jewellery apparently gifted to her by various tribe members the previous night. Furii shook her head and walked out, leaving Isabel to sort out her new accessories. She pretended to have no time for such things, but deep in the truck was a cigar box full of gifted tribal nick-nacks.

The rest of the tribe slowly started to gather around the low coals, waiting to be stoked into a new fire. Bomehari was collecting wood while Avari was giving some kind of blessing to the day-living humans of the tribe. Nakhari stood on the edge of the gathering, talking quietly to two men. When she saw Furii she gestured for her to join them, with some urgency.

'Furii my dear, this is Noveh and Valise. Noveh began work on your truck last night for Dinelae. Valise finished it through today and has completed the hidden box. It is a thing of genius, but unfortunately, I must press you to rush to Gamboori. The omens this morning spoke of a great battle that would become a massacre should you leave late.' Nakhari spoke low and quickly, fear thick in her voice. Furii didn't even ask how she knew such things. For Nakhari to be so panicked was unusual, so Furii just accepted the importance of the situation.

'Fine, I will grab Isabel and leave as soon as we can. Thank you both for all your efforts to modify the truck.' Furii turned to leave, but was stopped by Valise.

'Dinny had a few goodies spare to tweak ye truck too. Be noticin' some better speed on her and got ye a wee solar panel for desert trips. Nakhari said ye gonna be doing a lot more desert travel soon. So we got it self-sufficient like.'

'Oh, thank you. I will transfer you the bits later.'

'Naw, we done foraged them parts from a few rich folks that ain't be missing them. All even now.' Furii smirked at the implication of using the word 'foraging'. She nodded in response and strode off. Luckily, the tribes folk were not the most verbose people. They understood the inferred gratitude and had no need for platitudes.

Isabel had finally emerged from the seer's house and was watching Avari finish their blessings. Her head was cocked in fascination of these people so foreign to her life's experience. As soon as Furii approached Isabel felt the waves of tension rolling from her.

'Get your things, we have to go.'

'What happened? Did your bad attitude lose you friends again?'

'No. Ugh. Nakhari has foreseen the need for us to go now, or there will be some kind of massacre. We have to hurry, or many lives will be lost.' Furii spoke desperately, still striding into the Seer's House.

'Oh no. OK, I am onto it. I will get my things together, but gonna be sad to leave these people, they feel like family.' Isabel trotted inside and gathered up her sparse possessions, including a little care package Bomehari smuggled in for her. Furii was already jumping into the driver's seat by the time she came out. Nakhari and the apprentice seers were all present to see them off, along with most of the vampire tribe-kin. Their goodbyes were short but polite, with all present knowing the need for urgency.

The tribe disappeared into the dust of the wastelands as Furii headed for the point Nakhari had marked on their map. When they stopped to rest, Isabel tried out the newly crafted autophage smuggling chamber. She was delighted with the comfort, and Furii was delighted with the camouflage of the nook. It was entered via a concealed door in the bed of the truck, as far from the door as possible. They resumed their quest with much higher morale, excited by the prospects ahead. The emotions surrounding their need for a quick exit still swirled around the cabin. Both worried that they had doomed the tribe with their visit. Silent hopes were offered up that they had left soon enough that the danger passed.

Isabel gave no sarcastic comment, Furii barked no orders. They simply drove until the sun began to rise, remembering how aggressive the dawn felt in the desert. Locking down, they clambered into the back. It was only when lying in their beds that Isabel finally squeaked out a question.

'They will be fine, won't they?' Her voice shook with concern for her newfound friends. Furii was taken aback by her timidity.

'Despite their friendly ways, they are still a warrior tribe. I have even seen Nakhari herself fight with utter ferocity. Anyone who would wish to subdue them would have to put up a hell of a fight, and watch them all die before being subdued,' she answered carefully.

'But what about the ones who get taken like Gamboori?' Isabel asked curiously.

'The so-called servants are generally taken as children or infants, in flash raids. The private security for each family usually facilitates this. I have seen them moving out, a veritable small army. It's not right, but when those families have all the power, who is going to say no?' Furii asked dejectedly. Once again, she felt like she was defending the nobility she detested against this little anarchist.

'Lest Atlas shrug,' Isabel muttered under her breath, but Furii caught it.

'Who, who could fight them? The police? They are largely funded by those families. The bounty hunter ranks? Even if you could get them all to agree, most of the upper commanders come from, or are married to, the ruling families. Short of an uprising by common folk, it won't happen. Even then, they would have little chance against a well-equipped and well-trained miniature army... and that is only one family. The others would step in too, if not for love, then for the fact that they would be next.' Furii spoke to herself as much as Isabel. She hated seeing those genocidal teams march, but she was usually detached from it. Immersing herself in work was all she could do at this point.

Isabel fell into an unhappy silence. Neither felt up to breaking it with some kind of pithy platitude about the system, so they simply pondered their individual thoughts until sleep claimed them each in turn.

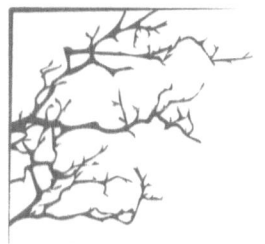

Chapter 12

The night sky burned a furious red, the stars eclipsed by the last spears of anger in the sun. They were close now. Furii felt it in her gut and confirmed it with the map. They would be in the area within a couple of hours. She dosed out the blood needed for a fight, taking extra to ensure fast healing if she needed it. Isabel took the same, and Furii was struck at how little grey there was in her skin now. Her ears were still pointed and her eyes remained resolutely grey and mottled. Isabel would still not pass as a vampire, but she was significantly better.

After their 'meal' settled, Isabel asked what the plan was.

'I will only be able to figure something out after I see this place and can see what we are up against. Roughly speaking, you stay behind me until I need you.' Furii spoke bluntly. Without knowing what defences were in place, Furii had no idea whether it was safe enough for Isabel to come along. As loath as she was to bring the little autophage in the first place, she also didn't want to be responsible for killing the kid. Luckily, Isabel nodded and didn't argue.

'Sure, you tell me what you need done and I am onto it,' she responded obediently. Silently, Furii pulled open her weapons kit and handed Isabel a gun and a knife, along with ammunition. Being guns suited for a vampire, the hand cannon made Isabel look even smaller, but she hefted it without issue.

'Know how to use it or need help?' Furii was gruff in her awkwardness.

'Nope,' Isabel responded as she checked the ammunition, grip and barrel before loading the weapon and removing the safety. She flipped the knife, checked the blade and nodded.

'How is some wasteland kid so proficient with weapons?'

'Firstly, I have been 9 for 120 years. Secondly, we weren't always in the wastes. My father and mother were both bounty hunters in the Tempest Rising clan. But Dad pissed off the wrong people, and we got poor. When my sister and my father started changing, we were forced to try our luck in the wastes. For a minute all was fine. We had a little group, all worked together on a farm. Then it all fell apart... Anyway, prior to all of that happening, my parents taught me everything I needed.' Isabel was lost in the memories, her voice flickering with emotion.

'Pissed off a family huh? Let's hope I don't make the same mistake. So, when we met, you could have given me a good fight?' Furii blurted out before remembering that was when she killed Isabel's parents. She sucked her lips in as soon as she realised, sealing her mouth up too late. Isabel snorted, well aware of the faux pas.

'Perhaps if you weren't beheading my sister. Might have given you the same treatment.'

'Do you ever want to?'

'We talked about this already. I knew they were gone. But I had held on. Hoped they would come back. Suddenly remember who I was. But they didn't, and they would have just eaten anyone else.' A small smile flittered across her lips as Isabel remembered a family long gone. Time with the tribe had mellowed her anger and given her a sense of grace.

Furii felt it was best to stay silent before she launched herself into greater trouble. Soon a series of low lights were visible on the horizon, enough to indicate a small populace. Pausing only to dim her own lights to hit barely a metre in front of the truck, Furii inched the grinding beast along. Finally, the risk of being seen was too great, so she pulled up off the dusty track. She needed to prepare for a frontal attack. Everything bought from Vincenza was packed within easy reach or given to Isabel. The little autophage was now bristling with weapons, silver eyes glimmering in the depths of the night. Furii felt an odd sense of nervousness, checking her comms pod again for the picture of the missing Gamboori. Warm brown skin, long brown hair, a dimpled smile. A birthmark staining the left-hand side of his neck. Every detail had been committed to memory. The Duchess Du Mort had sent another message reminding Furii of how little time she had to fulfil her task, and how all of the bandits must die. Every last one had to be killed in order to quash the criminal activity in the region. It was reiterated over and over again.

Furii felt sick to her stomach. Quickly shooting off a confirmation that she had seen the message felt like a betrayal, but Furii could not pinpoint why. Lacking any further option, she nodded to Isabel and climbed back into the cab to drive up to the hideout. Knowing that it was likely the group would see the vehicle coming, both Furii and Isabel had to be ready to hit the ground running.

This turned out to be entirely in the literal sense, as a hail of gunfire began as soon as they approached their destination. Furii swore loudly and shut her truck down, activating the daytime shields in an attempt to protect her beloved vehicle. They ran in a serpentine fashion, attempting to dodge the aim of the shooters. They managed to make it to the edge of the compound with only mild scrape hits from glancing shots.

The hearse was present, but a quick glance showed that they had siphoned off all the fuel, probably to fill one of the other cars. Short of refuelling it themselves, there was no way they would be reclaiming that one for the Duchess. They scuttled from vehicle to vehicle, checking for occupants or the items taken from the Du Mort manor. They came up empty-handed and turned to the main building. It looked like a decrepit warehouse that morphed into a bunker, corrugated metal joining the dunes.

Standing either side of metal doors crusted with neglect, Furii and Isabel alternated shooting in at the visible opponents. While Furii was an expert shot, she was still amazed at the precision with which Isabel picked off her targets. Within seconds the entrance room was clear, a warehouse-sized space now splattered with gore. Silence fell in the near environment, but running footsteps echoed from a distance. Isabel nodded at Furii and moved forward in a low crouch. Too surprised to admonish the kid, Furii watched her pick over the fallen, checking for supplies and survivors. This was a near professional at work, far from the mindless autophages wandering the wastes.

'Furii, we have a problem,' Isabel whispered as she leant over a body with pale legs sticking out of torn camo shorts.

'What? Don't tell me we shot the damn target!' Her response was a hiss of disappointment. That would be the cherry on top of this shit sandwich. Flicking a stray piece of carrion off the end of her gun, Furii stalked over angrily.

'Silver eyes. It's an auto.' Isabel didn't bother to whisper this time as the running feet drew closer. Furii glanced between her and the corpse, processing this information into a hell of a situation.

'Why would rampaging bandits have autos as part of their group? This shit is getting weirder- DOWN!' Furii stopped as a new group of weaponised men and women entered the room. They both dropped and rolled to cover as the first three interlopers shot wildly. There was something about the inept way they were shooting that rankled Furii. Regardless, she carefully selected her targets before doing away with finesse and skidding one of Vincenza's little pods into the centre of the fray. The resulting blast caused a storm of obsidian splinters to tear through the room. The shooters were taken by surprise, unable to even consider taking cover. They went down fast without landing a single shot on her or Isabel. Behind them there were more to join the fight. These people merely had bludgeoning weapons in the form of bats and pipes. They met an equal fate until the hall was clear. Furii shook her head at the mess of deceased vampires and autophages. She sniffed carefully, and Isabel mimicked her.

'Is that... human? Why would the humans be fighting, Furii? Weren't they supposed to be abducted?'

Furii confirmed what Isabel had detected. There was indeed human blood amongst the dead, with at least three of the bodies being human.

'These ones, they were the ones who had never handled a gun before. Those are the humans. These aren't lifetime bandits. They are just humans and autos. What is going on? We killed, what, 20 people, yet only 14 seemed to be experienced with weapons? There is something so wrong with this,' Furii muttered angrily. This was something so much more than what she had been told by the Du Morts. They checked over the bodies and soon found the Wintergrim uniform on a female combatant. The guard had not been abducted. The guard had joined them. A vampire guard allied to the Wintergrim estate was fighting with these humans and autophages. Furii and Isabel looked at each other dubiously. Shrugs were exchanged before they continued into the next rooms.

There was a long hall with a great many connecting doors. The sound of dripping water was the only tattoo to penetrate the silence. Methodically clearing each room, both women got crankier and crankier as they went. Each was horribly mundane, free from bars, restraints, torture items or even a locked door. There was human food set out, beds laid out for multiple people, ephemera and personal trinkets. There was an overall theme of equality and normalcy. It reminded them more of a pre-infection hippie commune. Still, Gamboori was nowhere to be seen. The third last room was some kind of common room, easily cleared and minimal fuss required. Finally, they found Gamboori behind the second last door, holding a gun in a trembling hand.

'Aww, come on human, don't make this harder for me. It's been a long night,' Furii muttered grumpily. Isabel dove out from behind her, arced across the wall and kicked Gamboori over in a single move. The gun fell to the floor without ever firing a shot. Furii gazed in awe at the little autophage.

Gamboori, on the other hand, was decidedly unimpressed.

'Why did you come here?' he asked snappily. Furii looked at him in confusion.

'What?'

'I would really rather stay here,' said the human.

'But... they kidnapped you?' she asked incredulously.

'Yep, sure, still better than with the Duchess. I went rather willingly. They even asked nicely.'

'Well, be that as it may, I am still tasked with returning you. The Duchess will end me if I return without her precious human.' Furii felt surly at needing to explain the importance of the situation.

'She couldn't care less, it is just her lost prestige due to being broken into. This is just a show of power. Quite a manipulation too.'

'What do you mean?' Isabel was ever the curious one.

'I mean-' Gamboori never bothered finishing as he reached for the gun. This time Furii was faster as she kicked it away, then spun into a back kick, knocking him out cold. She sighed.

'All of this is so wrong. I cannot believe that any of this is as it seems.'

'Not by the sounds of it. What will we do?' inquired Isabel, picking up the gun for herself. She checked the sight and the bullets, sniffed and shrugged before stashing it in her clothing. Furii placed cuffs on Gamboori.

'Take this – urgh heavy – fool back to the Duchess, get our pay and go.' Furii had winced as she hefted the man over her shoulder. Even with vampire strength, Gamboori was an enormous mass of muscle, all the heavier for being a dead weight. She slowly walked out, looking at the last door they had not cleared. Isabel watched for a decision.

Furii shrugged.

They had gotten what they had come for and had enough bloodshed. She did not want to bother with anything more than that. In exchange, Isabel covered their retreat out of the base, just in case someone did try to come from that room. Either it was empty, or they were smart enough to stay away. They made it back to the truck without any further intervention.

Gamboori was stashed into the back, with leg cuffs added and chained to the floor. Furii and Isabel would need to sleep in there, and there was no way they would allow him to bolt come sunrise or kill them in their sleep. Luckily, he could be chained at one end and they could sleep at the other, closer to the cabin.

When their prize was secure, Furii climbed into the driver's seat, Isabel beside her. Blood caps were handed out to begin healing, and wounds washed with pure water. They refreshed themselves in silence. Finally they felt more at ease, and Furii turned the beast for home. They drove on in silence as the rays of the sun began to crimson the sky.

'Blood has been spilt,' pondered Isabel sagely.

'No shit, kiddo.' Furii snorted sarcastically. They both allowed a grim chuckle.

To keep as much distance possible between them and the 'bandits', Furii left the daytime shields on and continued driving well into the morning. When she felt assured of their relative safety, she pulled the truck to a halt. As an extra precaution, she activated the motion sensors attached to an internal alarm. They were generally too sensitive in most places, but potentially being out in the abandoned desert with revenge-filled bandits on their tail, meant that she could justify their use.

'You did good. Really good. Today- kiddo.' Furii blushed into the compliment, unused to such words coming from her. Isabel nodded in return, content with not pushing her luck. Finally they both fell asleep, safely cloaked from the sun.

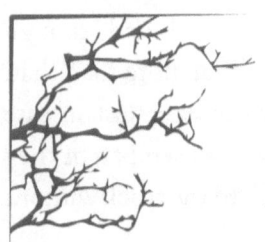

Chapter 13

The alarms blared, rousing both the vampires and a now loudly cussing Gamboori. He rattled his chains and glared at the women. They ignored him to grasp their guns and run into the cabin. The external videos showed autophages, eyes glittering in the night.

'It's a pack of ferals, Furii,' Isabel stated flatly. Thin hands with pointed nails grasped for the meagre light coming from the truck. Furii grabbed her sickles and guns, favouring her dual wield. Isabel took hers, with Gamboori's tucked into her belt as a back-up.

They nodded and Furii flipped the external lights on. The autophages were momentarily blinded, shying away from the light. This was their best chance, and they took it.

Furii and Isabel jumped out of their respective doors, guns a'blazing. They carefully picked each shot, despite the pack now turning to them and fighting blindly. Duck the claws and teeth, spring up, shoot. Dodge a blow, shoot. Run out of bullets, swap. Slice and cut, until they all lay dead. Isabel had taken a claw gash to the face, Furii had multiple scratches and bruises, but they had taken down 13 feral autophages. It alarmed Furii how much the two of them had synced up. Fighting was almost a dance between them.

'I guess you need your tags, huh? No sense wasting the loss,' Isabel pointed out. Furii was still too stunned to do more than nod. She fetched the tags from the cabin and began to organise the bodies. It would not be fun to carry the dead autophages for at least two days, given that they already stank, but the extra income for this little jaunt could buy a lot of fuel. She threw the back doors open to confront a glaring Gamboori.

'Just kill me now. Don't leave me with that, don't take me to the Duchess. Kill me. Consider it a favour,' he begged, looking at the dead autophages Furii and Isabel were dragging.

'Can't do that. Gotta get you back alive. It's in the contract.' Furii shut down any discussion there, but took care to pile the autophages as far away from Gamboori as possible. She also turned on the air purifier to keep the stench to a minimum. When all 13 had been tagged and loaded, they got back into the cabin. Furii silently handed out the blood caps and water, even throwing some fresh water to Gamboori in the back. He sulked, but took it anyway. Feeling cleaner and already starting to heal, they began driving again. The sands of the desert swallowed the blood, and small insects quickly took every last piece of flesh from the site. The tire marks were blown away, and soon nothing remained of the lives lost. The desert never changed for long.

A thought occurring to her, Isabel climbed into the back, carefully picking her way over the dead to sit by Gamboori.

'What do you want?' He growled and pulled at his chains, an exercise in futility.

'What was that place? Why are autophages, humans and vampires all being bandits together?' Isabel asked bluntly, loud enough for Furii to hear.

'Bandits? What the hell? No, kid, they are freedom fighters. Trying to protect the autophages that are cognizant still, and get the humans out of the city slavery.' He kept short of shouting, but not by much. Isabel flinched.

'Furii was told they are dangerous bandits kidnapping humans for food and trade. The Duchess threatened her. The tribe-kin even saw a slaughter of her and the tribe if she did not comply.' Isabel spoke lower, but Furii heard it. The kid had known more than she was letting on then.

'Well I can't help that. What you two destroyed was a chance at freedom, from the tyranny of the families, murder clans and false government. You decimated a main line, but at least a few survived I bet. Unless you guys torched the place after I was knocked out. Wouldn't surprise me. Was there a bonus to blow the place up? To annihilate the entire camp?' He was trying to inflame the women, but got no push back.

'No,' responded Isabel flatly. 'We left the last room and the base intact. I am sure we were supposed to, but we didn't. There was something too wrong about it all. Especially the autos. Everyone in the city wants us dead, but the tribes and others are fighting for us?'

'What do you mean, the city wants you dead?' Gamboori was now curious, despite his inherent belligerence.

'Furii was ordered to kill me. To cover up my existence. The city pretends there are no conscious autophages. They use it to generate fear and keep the bounty hunter clans in jobs. My parents were part of all of that before their downfall. Heck, the only reason I am a phage now is because my parents pissed off the wrong family. But now, Furii saved me. She protected me from that kind of death. She risked everything. Hate her for filling out her orders if you like, under threat of death, but not for who she is.' Isabel patted Gamboori on the knee and stood carefully with the swaying of the vehicle. She fished some human food out of a stash she had received from the tribe for Gamboori and handed it over. He took it thankfully and sat thinking everything over as he ate.

Isabel returned to the front, nodding to Furii as the only communication. Somehow the kid looked almost healthy for a vampire. Her hair was growing back, her claws were almost normal nails. Furii was amazed at the change in the girl, both mentally and physically. She drove on in silence but was comforted by her words.

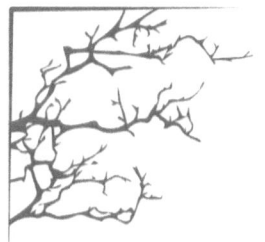

Chapter 14

The night, as well as the next day's sleep, proved uneventful. Gamboori had stopped trying to annoy the vampires and preventing their sleep, choosing to believe the stories spoken by Isabel. There was little else he could do. The dead autophages raised a stink, the flesh of such a cold-blooded predator decomposing faster than the average. Furii could have closed off the back of the truck to the cabin, but she didn't want to trap Gamboori in with them alone. They blasted the air purifier as best they could but were all over the stench. Finally, they just dragged Gamboori into the cabin with the promise that he would behave, then sealed off the bed. Fully closed, the refrigeration could be used to preserve the bodies better.

The night of driving proved to be uneventful, with shared tales and small patches of gossip littering the dark hours. Furii even allowed Isabel to attempt driving in a particularly flat and desolate part of the desert, which terrified Gamboori. Isabel's squeals of joy were almost drowned out by Gamboori's shouts of fear every time the truck lurched from side to side.

'You bloody vampires might survive an accident, but I am a human! I need self preservation!'

'I thought you wanted to die anyway!' argued Isabel in a joking manner. The three were starting to embrace gallows humour together. Seeing his white knuckle grip on the chair convinced Isabel to relinquish control, handing the captain's seat back to Furii.

They managed to make it to the next morning without a barking contest or accident, and all three opted to sleep in the cabin rather than risk the stench and chill of the back. The day passed uneventfully, and they all managed to secure some sleep. Unfortunately, the warmth of the day still managed to heat up the truck, despite the extensive insulation measures. The relief felt when they all awoke and could finally open the windows was well-expressed in a variety of sighs and expletives.

Anticipating her return to the city and getting the putrid bodies out of her truck as soon as she could manage, Furii set off early, forgoing the breakfast. After a few kilometres, Isabel quietly got up and braved the back to get to the fridge. The smell was bad enough, but the fluids leaking from the bodies and congealing in the cold was something else entirely. The autophage gagged; despite having seen far worse in the wasteland, she certainly hadn't smelt worse.

Regardless, they needed to feed, and Isabel battled the stench all the way to the fridge. Climbing back into the cab, she handed the donated human food to Gamboori, then dosed out the blood. As Isabel passed Furii her dose, she held her hand up to refuse the offering.

'Pass.' She muttered, as curtly as possible.

'If you don't feed now, you will be feral by sunup. We need you to have full control.' The autophage chastised the bounty hunter. Amusement rippled through Furii's stern countenance. She dutifully held out her hand for the offered caps. The kid was right- she had yet to smuggle an autophage back into the city, get a human back to the evil overlords and get putrefying bodies out of her beloved truck. The thought alone made her head pound.

Furii drove for as long as she could stand, but before midnight she was forced to stop. Every move ached, and it felt as though her brain was threatening to violently exit her skull. The truck door squealed loudly as she threw it open, protesting her violence. Gulping in fresh air held back a full physical response, but it was enough to send shudders through her body. In all of her centuries as a vampire, Furii had never vomited. For her body to be giving such a visceral response now, she was more than a little worried.

Isabel came around the truck to help Furii, just in time for a feral autophage to come screeching out of the liquid black depths of a wasteland night. Drawing a knife, Isabel dropped into a low crouch.

She was coiled to strike.

The autophage continued towards Furii blindly. He was either oblivious to Isabel's alteration into a deadly fighting stance or simply did not care. His bloodlust and violence gave him pure tunnel vision.

Before Furii could react herself, the head of the feral autophage was rolling around on its chest, attached by a scant few strands of muscle and skin. The body dropped slowly, or perhaps the adrenalin flooding their senses made it seem so.

Furii couldn't help but sigh. Despite it earning her more bits, now there was another autophage to add to the stinking pile. Her truck was becoming a veritable tumbril. Unfortunately, even if they dumped the bodies out, the stench would remain until they could get to the city and deep clean the beast. So Furii tagged the new autophage and threw it in the back.

They collectively decided that they would stay in their current position for the night. None particularly wanted to delay their travel and consequent freedom from the taphonomic wonderland in the truck, but nor did any want to rush back to the city.

Furii sat and pondered her dilemma of being puppeteered into slaughtering a group of freedom fighters on behalf of the much-despised controlling families. Isabel wondered about her future, being snuck in and out of the city and killing her own kind. Gamboori lamented being returned to the Du Mort manor and giving up his small measure of freedom. The melancholy hung in the air, yet none dared to speak and dissipate its grasp for hours.

The sun was breaking the horizon when Gamboori finally shattered the silence with a plea.

'Don't take me back. You have fuel, we can just keep running until we are out of the reach of the Du Morts. Please, you would be returning me to hell.'

Furii looked at Isabel, and the silence stretched on again as they desperately tried to read each other's mind.

'We can do it.'

'We could never do it,' said Isabel and Furii at the same time. It was Furii who held up a hand to silence all discourse.

'The Duchess Du Mort paid me a disgustingly high amount of money to find you and a car. They will easily front more money to have me killed, and you returned by the next bounty hunter. They will also slaughter an entire tribe from pettiness.'

'It wasn't for me. They would never pay that much for a slave, especially one from the tribes.'

'A slave? You are a human, a necessity to survive as vampires.' Furii couldn't help but feel unsure in her words, and the trepidation leaked into her voice.

'There are well over 200 humans in that miniscule building. That many for one bitch and her 'honoured guests' is ridiculous. This is not about me, it's about the freedom fighters and their habit of liberating slaves from the controlling families,' Gamboori explained, with frustration darkening his inflections.

'No, she gave me her word, as I gave mine. It will work out,' Furii insisted. That insistence, however, did not stop the doubts from insidiously weaving into her thoughts. Isabel chose to keep quiet.

'Well, your word has resulted in the death of our hope. Live with that.' His final words punched into an uneasy existence. With that, he turned his back, feigning sleep.

'I'm so sorry.' Isabel spoke to no one in particular. Knowing both sides of this argument, she offered up a futile apology out of desperation. Furii shook her head sadly.

'I am used to that. If I don't give you back, they will kill me. It's been done before. They were no doubt prepared to kill Nakhari's tribe. If I don't play along, we all probably die, knowing about the autophages. All of it is a big ol' mess.' Furii saw some of the tension ease in Gamboori, but he still refused to speak.

Isabel played with the last of her blood capsules thoughtfully while they spoke.

'Ever learnt not to play with your food?' Furii teased to lighten the mood.

'Why do you take these rather than just drinking?' Isabel asked innocently. The entire atmosphere around Furii darkened in seconds. This was her taboo, never having passed her lips since being taken in by the Hellstorm clan.

'It's... not a fun tale. You sure you want to know?'

'You let me talk about my family, we can share such burdens.' Isabel held the sad gaze of the bounty hunter, meeting her eyes with honesty and integrity. Gamboori held silent, comprehending the importance of the conversation. Furii sighed and scratched the stubble on the side of her head.

'I was one of the last to get infected during the first generation crisis. The outbreak lasted 20 years as an avalanche of infections, before the spread slowed. I was attacked in year 2 post-outbreak by a man seeking revenge for his own infection, by infecting as many innocent people as possible. He was put down shortly after.' Furii exhaled slowly. Tension engulfed her body as the memories scrolled by.

'We knew so little, even after 22 years. I was patched up after the initial attack, then sent home with a 'Now you're a vampire' pamphlet and no real clue. I thought I only had to feed as much as the vampires I had seen at work. I grew hungrier to the point of hallucinations. I thought it was all part of the infection. I went home... and had a normal night with my fiancé, while our toddler played nurse.' Furii choked on tears she was ashamed of. She felt as though she had no right to mourn a loss she had caused.

'I attacked them. My partner, my *child*. I tore into the ones I love. When I woke up, all I could taste was... them. The lifeblood of my family. They were... shredded. It was like a sleepwalking incident, I remembered nothing. It wasn't until I woke up that I saw the extent of it. Those frail little bodies, even the bulk of my massive partner was gone. Instead, there was a small mound of flesh. The taste of old blood poisoned my mouth. Blood and flesh.' Furii was forced to stop there. Isabel and Gamboori were shocked into silence.

Furii held back her tears as best she could, but the blood still dripped from her eyes. She wiped at it with her sleeve. Soon she gave in to the sobs.

Isabel jumped at the wails of the hunter. The scarred bounty beast was sobbing into her hands. Neither had seen Furii like this. Isabel hesitated before putting a thin arm around the older vampire. Slowly she eased to a sniffle.

'Sorry, got the morbs.' Furii attempted to dismiss the emotional outbreak with feigned ease. Awkward laughs were shared, all present were intensely uncomfortable with overt emotions. The vampire and the autophage soon resumed some banal banter to dismiss the mood. Gamboori remained relatively quiet, pondering all that he had learned about the killer of his saviours. The sheer complexity of emotions left him paralysed in analysis.

'Tomorrow night we should be able to make it back to the city, only about 140 kilometres out. Will drop Gamboori off, then I gotta collect my bounty and sneak Isabel into home.' Furii turned to the autophage. 'I am sorry you will have to spend so long in the compartment, but I don't want to risk someone seeing you in the mansion. They have an army of droogs just waiting to kill something.' Her voice was almost soft. Normally as harsh as the mocking of a raven, Isabel was struck mute by the sentiment in Furii's voice.

'Ah, yeah sure, I get it,' Isabel muttered gruffly as she settled down in her makeshift bed. Furii took the chance to ease her awkwardness and bedded down for the night too. Eventually only Gamboori was awake, deep into the day, ruminating on all he had seen and heard. For once it did not occur to him to kill Furii and escape.

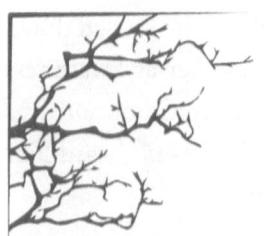

Chapter 15

The moon rose, and so did the bloodsuckers. Furii roused first, but lay in bed pondering the wisdom of sharing her story the previous night. Isabel she could trust, but Gamboori would shortly be delivered to the Duchess. There was no telling what may happen with a rumour of her weakness circulating. Whether voluntarily or under duress, Gamboori now had the ability expose one of Furii's tightly-clutched secrets. The thought made her sick. Such information could be a formidable weapon.

Isabel began to slowly stir, so Furii was forced to get out of her bed roll and look nonplussed. There was an almost comfortable silence as they had breakfast together, in a manner of speaking. Blood caps were handed out, more stashed human food given and surface pleasantries abounded. Gamboori eased off taunting Furii, and both kept a kinder tone. Regardless of the attempt at normalcy, the gloom was still pendulous. As soon as the sun had fully set, they put every window down. Better to risk a swarm of autophages than to smell their rotting corpses. Even the newest one was beginning to swell rapidly.

When they were 20 kilometres out of the city, Furii stopped the truck and carefully surveyed their surroundings. When she was confident that there was no one in their proximity to see what she was doing, Furii sealed Isabel away in her secret compartment. For the sake of theatre, she also restrained Gamboori again. The rest of the drive to the city was done white knuckled, tension evident in her gritted jaw and darting looks.

Upon reaching the gates to the city, Furii glanced at Gamboori and nodded sympathetically. He averted his eyes, refusing to acknowledge the implied apology. The guards checked the usual parts of the van, but upon smelling the rancid bodies in the bed of the truck, they simply waved them through. *Small mercies,* Furii thought as she took the roads leading up to the Du Mort manor.

As much as she wanted to drop the bodies off first, Furii had no doubt that the Duchess would be tracking her vehicle. It seemed to be the thing to do lately.

The security officers at the mansion were equally disgusted by the smell of the vehicle, but managed to at least open the doors and inspect that there was no one living in the back. Furii was instructed to park as far from the mansion as possible, lest they stink up the occupants. This part was intensely entertaining to her, and she pushed that boundary with glee. While driving up the excessively long driveway, Furii tested the wind, and made sure to park upwind of the main entrance. A butler came hurrying out.

'Hunter Furii of the Hellstorm clan, I... ugh!' The usually stoic hired help now retched aggressively, panic in his eyes. He barely looked at Gamboori, instead making fast moves towards the main door. As soon as we had cleared the threshold, he slammed it closed aggressively to attempt to block out the stench. Furii couldn't help but grin. This was the level of petty she adored. Again she was led through the warren of hallways to a closed set of beautifully ornate doors. There were clear sounds of a party beyond.

Sniffing herself delighted Furii even more. With too many days on the road, a battle zone and time spent with rotting autophages, she smelled utterly ripe. The richest of vampire society were about to be olfactorily assaulted. Gamboori did not return the goofy smile. The doors were thrown open, and Furii strode in, wafting her stench through the room. The most hideous glares were shot back in response, but none dared speak now that Furii and the Duchess had locked eyes.

'Duchess, I have returned your human to you.'

'Very good. Take it to the stable with all the other cattle, then clean up and you may join us.'

'The cattle?' Furii chided, stifling a sneer before the Duchess noticed.

'Yes, around the back. You have already been there, nosing about. I am sure you can find a stable-hand or something to take that thing.'

That was the moment that Furii realised Gamboori had been correct. His return was just a small bonus for her having eradicated any chance at fighting the Du Morts and their vampire elite, as well as stifling the secret of the special autophages.

He was right. She was wrong.

She had killed so many people based upon this lie.

The silence had stretched on for far too long. Gamboori subtly tugged at his end of the restraints, reminding Furii that she had been given an order and was now being watched carefully. She simply chose to nod at the Duchess, then leave.

'You simply cannot train the lower classes to be anything but trash...' Furii heard her intone pointedly, to the roars of laughter. The thoughts in her mind were a massive crushing avalanche, tearing sanity from its moorings. Gamboori was smart enough to hold silent.

As soon as they left the main mansion, Furii muttered tersely. 'Give me two nights. Be ready.' She didn't even look over at him. There was no point. She could feel the elation, hear the rapid beat of his heart kicking into overdrive. When Gamboori was handed off to the stable hand, who much more resembled a prison guard, Furii began to take note of people and weapons. She counted carefully, memorising every window and door. Every detail was cemented into her mental layout.

This time Furii was shown to a small bathroom in the servants' quarters, which suited her just fine. This was likely the best way in. There was a great deal of soap, a threadbare towel and a servant's uniform placed out for her, a none-too-subtle hint. Furii took as much time as she dared to, knowing that Isabel was still stuck in the compartment. Even with her many books, it would not be easy. Scrubbed from top to toe, Furii had to admit she did feel better.

Finally, the staff were convinced that Furii was at least clean enough to return to the party. She accepted a drink she had no intention of touching before sidling back over to the Duchess Du Mort.

'Why didn't you tell me...' Furii started, but was interrupted by every head in the room turning toward her and a sharp look from the Duchess Du Mort.

'Tell you what, little killer?' She spoke with a maniacal grin. The spider was now looking down on its little trapped fly. Furii realised that the Duchess was looking for a reason to have her killed. There would be no fighting her way out of this one, in a room full of her peers and several armed thugs.

'That he was such a looker, but such a pain in the ass. How do you cope with all that talking?' she asked, puffed up with mock bravado. It seemed to stick, the Duchess roaring with laughter.

'My darling killer, that is why you beat them until they cannot talk. Eventually the poor dim creatures learn. That one was particularly hard, however. Part of why I am so fond of it. Took some taming, but the blood was divine. It lacked the fear you get so often with these beasts.' Her voice was the poisoned steel knife, hidden in the milk and honey. It allured and disgusted in equal volumes. Furii just agreed silently. The sooner she got her money, the sooner she could leave.

Furii swirled her drink, watching the bubbles dance over the subtle oil sheen of poison. It was time to go. They were all eyeing her hungrily, waiting for her inevitable collapse.

'Well Duchess, I have impinged upon your delightful soiree for long enough. If you would be so kind as to transfer the rest of those bits to my account, I shall not bother you again.' Furii let a little of the drink slosh out of the glass, making sure the Duchess saw the outrageously red liquid splash onto her perfectly clean beige carpet. Furii pretended to take a long drink from the glass, without letting the liquid touch her lips, a method taught to the beginner bounty hunter. Many had been poisoned by drinks offered from a 'grateful' contractor. So much so that it became standard to teach all apprentices how to detect and avoid poison.

There was a tense stand-off before the Duchess Du Mort simply smiled slowly, and gestured with her hand. Within a minute, the silence was torn by a subtle beep from Furii's comms pod, notifying her that the money was in.

'Well, I thank you greatly for the ease of this little business deal. If you will excuse me, I have a van of dead autos that I must cash in on.' Furii made her voice and words as coarse as possible. Members of the listening crowd actually winced.

'Oh, don't let me keep you from your little errands of death. You deserve the most there.' The Duchess Du Mort was bitter, and it showed on her face. Checking the carpet one last time revealed it being eaten away in slow bubbles by the poison spilt upon it. By now the feverish crowd would expect her insides to be liquid. Alas for their blood glee, Furii safely managed to leave the mansion, striding confidently towards the truck. There was still every possible chance that a sniper had been procured to finish Furii off in case the poison did not, but no death pellets rained down. As an added touch, she made sure to feign extreme pains while driving through the security checkpoint.

They were out.

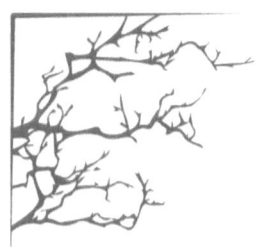

Chapter 16

Not willing to risk stopping and checking on Isabel, Furii just had to hope she was surviving in there. The Sheriff was the final stop, to unload the tagged autophages and collect the last money she would earn in this city. The Sheriff's office seemed to be aware she was approaching, which was no surprise. It was clear she was tracked, and there was a general sense of wariness. As Furii drove into the drop-off zone, she could swear she saw the Sheriff's trigger finger itch. He was surrounded by his usual goons, and sweat was in abundance. Their gaze prickled into Furii as she stepped out of the cab. Tempted to put her hands or at least a single finger up, Furii opted to simply act clueless.

'Hellstorm, you have returned from the Duchess Du Mort's mission. How- er, how did that go?' The sheriff mumbled nervously. Furii nodded quietly, not willing to waste the breath to respond. He was inspecting Furii carefully, and she was sure that he was looking for signs of poisoning.

The sheriff looked at each of his men in turn. When he nodded, they moved to the back of Furii's truck and opened the doors. At least two retched, and one ran for a pole to puke behind. Furii just grinned.

'I gotta admit, I generally think you women aren't cut out for sheriff-in', but I see things like this and it shows how vicious you all are.' The smirk smeared across his obese face was full of patronising intent. Furii sighed, but the sheriff continued to dig. 'Especially you darker ones, normally your kind only work hard to get a man to leech off, but you, you are sure unique.' The man wheezed with the effort of pushing his enormous, sweat-slick bulk away from his idle lean against the work bench. Furii ignored the casually racist comment, simply filing it away in her mind as another check mark against the sheriff.

'Boss, please don't make us...' One of the men tried to protest, but was cut off by the Sheriff.

'You rookies better get onto it. You, Hellstorm, come with me.' The sheriff grunted out the orders, all the while indicating to Furii to follow him to his office. Furii stalled, afraid of the rookies finding Isabel in her compartment. A louder grunt and an inaudible muttered word spurred her on. All Furii could hope for was that Isabel was capable of defending herself. She had left the autophage with enough weapons to give any attacker hell.

Back to that awful drab office, with its stench of sweat and deception. The sheriff crashed his ungainly bulk into his chair and sighed, eyeing Furii over. Despite being a putrid genocidal bigot, he was still smart enough to calculate the risk of her. Furii tried to look nonchalant and non-threatening. The guns and sickles over black body armour did not help.

'So you have completed a mission for the Duchess Du Mort and brought me more dead autophages. Anything unusual that you noticed?' he asked bluntly. Direct it was, then.

'Yes, they were sentient again. I tagged the ones I got on the road, but clearing out that mess in the desert would have taken too long. Thought it was best to leave them there to rot underground, where no one could find them.' She conveniently left out the part where at least one room of people was left untouched. The sheriff leaned back against his long-suffering chair.

'So you killed them and left them. Not ideal, but it will do. I could transfer more if you had tagged and returned them. Good for poking 'n prodding by 'em scientists. Still, will pay fer the ones you did return.' The sheriff watched Furii carefully for a moment, hoping she would collapse, and he would not have to pay out the money for her kills. When no weakness was shown, he sighed again and transferred the bounty. For the second time today, her comms pod beeped to show a large transfer. Furii smiled with gritted teeth, wary as ever.

Poor Isabel was still stuck in the truck filled with rotting autophage flesh, and this man seemed determined to stall her. Putting on what she hoped equated to an amicable smile, Furii tried to set up an imminent exit.

'Well Sheriff, lovely as always. I will be heading out to claim my next bounties in the next few days. I will talk to you later.' She stood, making sure that every move was purposeful and slow. The Sheriff's trigger finger was itching up a storm. His hands trembled over his ridiculously large gun. Furii hoped that impotence applied to those tense fingers too, and only relaxed when she made it back to the basement.

The truck stood abandoned, all bodies removed, although no attempt had been made to clean all of the fluids. Isabel was nowhere to be seen, so Furii had to simply hope that they had not found her. She jumped into the driver's seat and took off as fast as her caution could allow. Everything had to seem normal for two days. All hell could, and would, break loose in two days, no sooner.

Pulling into her own home was a relief. Furii closed the garage doors as quickly as possible, then ran to free Isabel. The smell was indescribable, flesh and putrefaction tinged with the rust of blood and metal. The decomposing autophages had begun to corrode the floor of the truck. The second that Furii released the hidden hatch, Isabel jumped out of her cocoon. Even for an autophage, she looked pale.

'I don't think I can ever truly communicate how vile that experience was. Even with moving the bodies, the bile from them leaked through and burnt my arm. Please don't ever make me do that again,' Isabel begged, showing an arm both covered in purge fluid and blood. Furii felt waves of guilt washing away her ability to speak.

'I... I am... I tried,' she stammered in a futile attempt at communication. Isabel put her good hand on Furii's shoulder.

'I get it, but right now I desperately need a shower and a bandage,' she said gently, as her blood continued to drip to the floor. Furii took the cue, running to prepare everything Isabel needed. While she was cleaning up, Furii took the time to thoroughly clean out her truck before airing it out as best she could in the closed garage.

The hot-cold roller coaster of her shower still felt blissful after so many days of travel and warfare. Furii luxuriated in her second shower of the day for far longer than she had intended, ensuring every bit of blood and grime was cleansed. She took the extended scrubbing time to start working on a plan for the promised two days.

When Furii emerged from the bathroom, Isabel was already asleep on the couch. The autophage now had a silver halo of hair growing out, and normal hands, despite their silver tones. Only a handful of days with regular feeding and she was beginning to pass as a regular vampire.

Furii briefly wondered if the ruling families knew that rehabilitation was possible, but she doubted that they cared enough to investigate.

Before collapsing into bed herself, Furii ordered a small fortune in blood capsules to be delivered ASAP, then set an alarm to go and visit Vincenza. She was going to need every trick she could muster to pull this off.

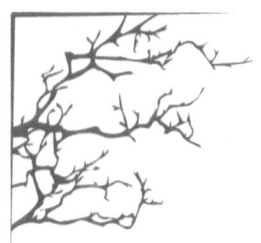

Chapter 17

The blaring was infuriating. An alarm, screeching in her ear. Furii cussed and moaned before remembering why she had set the alarm. It was time to work. There was an almighty battle to be planning, She would have to do some of her best work to survive this and to save the humans.

A check in with Isabel had the plan shared, and her eagerness was clear. Next Furii had to contact Nakhari, who was clearly expecting her call. Her congenial tones soothed Furii's tension as she answered.

'Well hello killer, got a need to chat or shall we get to this rather distressing news that the spirits scream into my ear?' the seer said by way of greeting.

Furii didn't even bother acting surprised.

'I have to get Gamboori out of there. I plan on releasing as many of the others that I can. Then I head for the desert and the rest of those left at the hideout.'

'By doing so, the city will wage war on my tribe and murder us all,' Nakhari stated, without exaggeration or flair. This was a simple fact, shared amongst blood sisters.

'You have seen this, so I suppose we must plan for it. But I told Gamboori that I would come for him in two days. They called the humans cattle, Nakhari.' Furii felt an emotional outburst threaten to erupt, her voice choking. It was hard to breathe.

'They do, they come to raid us for wild raised stock, remember? Go get him, and as many as you can save, then meet me at the location you found Gamboori.' Nakhari advised. Furii was shocked.

'Meet you there? But what about the tribe? The Du Morts will surely attack soon after whether I am successful or not.' As much as she needed Nakhari's aid, Furii could not endanger the tribe.

'My dear, the tribe has been packing up for the last two days. Many have already left to go to the meeting point. We realise that it is time to move away from the city.' The seer was endlessly practical in her leadership. Furii choked back tears.

'I am sorry to make you move, but I will be there, and I will fight for your people.' She blurted out the words in a jumble, before disconnecting the call abruptly. Furii had never been good with emotions, especially when she felt plagued by guilt.

Now to the second task. As Furii shoved a handful of blood caps in her mouth, she instructed Isabel to discreetly and quietly start packing. It was time to see Vincenza.

Entering the Hellstorm compound for what was probably the last time felt oddly correct. While under the guise of a family clan, the Hellstorm organisation was none too different from a corporation. The bounty hunters were all good little employees, making the tithes taken for raising unwanted children and turning them into elite vampire bounty hunters. Furii found that she was just unable to care anymore, all illusions irreparably shattered. One little autophage with the tempest in their eyes had woken Furii from her lethargy. Part of her missed the apathy, the voided empathy.

Unfortunately, life rarely allowed such nonsense to continue.

Loading up with everything that could go "bang", Furii made sure to grab all of Vincenza's excellent explosive pods. Money really was no object thanks to her ill-gotten gains. All those digital bits would be worth nothing in the wasteland, so she had to splurge. Money meant squat in the face of survival. Bombs would make better companions. Vincenza seemed a little surprised at Furii's spend up, but knew better than to question it. A bounty hunter buying that much ammunition and explosives was one to be left in peace.

Loading the many heavy crates into her truck gathered the curious gaze of other Hellstorm members, but Furii ignored it. She also stopped by the blood dispensary for the Hellstorm clan. Normally Furii avoided it as it was far cheaper to order the capsules to be delivered, but she wanted to cover up the fact that she was buying enough blood for an exodus into the wasteland.

Cleaning them out of caps at the Hellstorm compound only brought some mildly curious looks, as the hunters often needed more provisions for long hunts.

As she was pulling out onto the main driveway, Furii stopped and stepped out of the car and took one last look at the various buildings that she had spent so long in. While she had not grown up there, she had spent many long years being tortured with bounty hunter training and essentially indentured servitude.

Still, there was a sense of nostalgia to it all. Furii had been a feral mess when she arrived here, having just eaten her family. Being shuttled off to the Hellstorms was some kind of penance for her crimes, and they had formed her into the perfect killer of autophages. She had felt a sense of home. Now a little autophage had forced Furii to open her eyes, and it was time to turn those skills against their system. The nostalgic thoughts were a beautiful lie. Furii soon became aware of her position. Standing in the middle of the road and acting weird was an excellent way to tip people off that Furii was up to something.

Isabel had done a remarkable job of packing- almost all of Furii's sparse belongings had been carefully wrapped in whatever the kid could find. The whole lot was piled by the door to the garage, save for what they needed during the day's rest. Furii showed her gratitude before tiredly walking to her bedroom. The plan had to be perfect.

It was Isabel and Furii versus a private army.

It would not be easy.

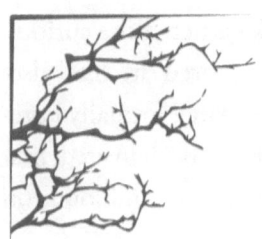

Chapter 18

Saying goodbye to her derelict villa was easy enough for Furii, since she had never really cared for the place besides the independence it offered. The last of her bits had been spent on an over-day delivery of goods to take with them, spare clothes, toiletries and even some new books for Isabel. The autophage squealed with excitement, but was less enthused about the wig Furii had ordered for her. While she understood the need, Isabel was reluctant to hide her autophage nature while in town.

'It's as itchy as a camel's ass in the desert,' she whined. Furii grinned at the analogy.

'They haven't existed since the fall. How would you know?'

'I read!' Shot back the belligerent teen.

Furii laughed as she packed the last items into her truck, making sure they were packed well to the front to ensure maximum space for passengers.

Her mirth dimmed as she remembered the tracker placed on her truck. Isabel noticed the sudden change in atmosphere and stopped to query it.

'The tracker. The sheriff will be able to see us make a move on the Du Mort manor. Where would it be? The freaking guards will be hard enough without the law enforcement joining the party.' While Furii was pondering, Isabel began to rummage around in the few boxes they were leaving.

'You mean this?' she asked, holding up a small capsule device. Furii was astounded.

'When did you... how did you know?' The confusion and awe made the hunter flustered, a condition she was not used to at all. Isabel laughed without derision.

'I read.' With that, the kid threw the tracker back into the box, slapped the wig onto her head and started loading up her new guns. The little autophage she found at the end of her gun in the desert was a wonder.

Furii had to ponder what her parents had been like. She realised that she had never taken the time to ask Isabel any more about them, their hunter clan and so on. Now was not the time to be engaging in a deep and meaningful discussion, but Furii tried to note it to ask later.

They were packed, armoured and ready.

It was time.

The ride over to the manor was grim, and this time Furii even opted to wear her helmet. There could be no chance for an errant head shot, or she would be leaving Isabel in the hornet's nest alone. Who knew what disgusting experiments they would execute on the poor kid if they caught her?

'Stop fiddling with it, kiddo.' Furii chastised Isabel as she scratched furiously at her wig.

'Furii, I am hundreds of years old. I am not a kid.' The sheer teenage belligerence in Isabel's demeanour gave Furii even more of a laugh.

'Well aware. Shit!' Furii swore loudly as she pulled into view of the Duchesses manor and realised there were two sheriff's cars at the front gate. They seemed to be vacated, but this was certainly a complication.

Spanner, meet works.

As Furii slowed down to take in the view, Isabel cheekily shot the two guards. Nothing fatal for a vampire, but enough to take them out of the fight. Thanks to the reinforced front bar and a lead foot, the truck easily smashed through the front gate. This drew the attention of the rest of the guards within earshot, and they swarmed in. Furii nodded at Isabel as they careened up the long driveway, kicking up pebbles as she looped around the fountain in front of the mansion.

By the time the guards reached them on foot, they had reversed up to the 'stable' and were ready for them.

Despite coming from all directions, each guard was shot or otherwise incapacitated before they managed to get a clear shot of their own. Soon the area was littered with bodies and the perfect grass ruined with scorch marks and pits. Furii took a moment to breathe, interrupted by a bullet ploughing into her chest armour and knocking her down.

'Sniper!' Shouted Isabel as she took off in the direction of the shot. Furii dragged herself behind her truck for shelter as another shot tore through the pebbles on the road she had vacated. Quickly checking if anything was terminal, it looked like her armour had saved her again. Still, she was going to have a lot of impact damage to recover. Brushing off the debris, Furii lurched up into a crouch. After a few seconds more shots rang out, followed by a loud and meaty thud. Isabel screamed out into the night.

'Got her. Clear this side.' Wherever the kid was, she was up high, and Furii wondered how she had achieved that in mere seconds. This was not the time to reflect, however. She quickly shot at two more guards running in from the gloom but missed one. A sniper shot zipped over her head, and the guard she had missed crumpled to the floor. Isabel had taken up the sniper post, giving Furii the best chance she had to free the humans. As Isabel picked off any more new arrivals, Furii tested the door carefully. She was fully expecting an ambush. The door was locked, of course, so she gathered all of her vampire strength to body slam it. The rough wooden door frame buckled before splintering inwards, taking a massive deadbolt with it. These people had been locked in.

The internal lights momentarily blinded Furii, being a nighttime predator. As her vision cleared, she was able to take in her surroundings. As opposed to the ostentatious opulence of the main mansion, this was akin to a 1700's peasant property. Everything was plain, rough wood and broken. She tried to take in her surroundings as fast as possible, assessing every shadow for threats. The room was empty, but Gamboori's head soon poked around the other doorway entering this room. He was clearly relieved to see her, and fully entered the foyer. Bruises tracked up each limber arm, turning his tanned skin a mottled purple. His face was viciously maimed with four deep fingernail wounds.

Despite his wounds, he led the other humans out, all carrying packs. Furii felt a crippling sense of guilt when she saw the fresh injuries many of them bore. There was also far less than the 200 Gamboori had quoted. If only she could have prepared faster. Still, Gamboori stopped beside her with a weak smile.

'Thank you, for keeping your promise,' he kept his voice low but audible, a weary growl. 'I got them all to pack this time, we were waiting for you.'

'But what if I hadn't made it? The Duchess tried to poison me that day.' Furii responded, surprised at his faith in her.

'Then we were going to end it all. Fight back or die trying.' His face earnest yet serious, Gamboori spoke clearly of their desperation.

Furii nodded in return, turning to direct the humans towards her truck. They filed out, smart enough to keep low and move quickly. Gamboori counted them off as they left, satisfied they had all made it out. Furii threw open the back doors and the humans all piled in, filling the space closest to the cab.

The last had gotten in safely, so "ambo'ri began to jog over too. It was when he drew level with the side door to the main mansion that it slammed open, destroying the rendering on the wall and shattering the glass. The repugnant sheriff popped out and grabbed Gamboori, dragging him inside before Furii could even consider reacting. Despite being a fat lump, he still had vampire strength behind him.

Swearing loudly, Furii shouted to the stowed humans that she was going after him and slammed the armoured doors of the truck closed to keep them safe. They locked automatically and all shields were down, so no one was getting in without the key she or Isabel bore.

Running through the maze of hallways was easier to navigate this time. Gamboori had made sure to kick, scuff or destroy every wall and art piece while being dragged through. Following the Hansel and Gretel trail of destruction led to a smaller greeting room, Gamboori on his knees and four of the sheriff's best with guns drawn and pointed at her. The sheriff himself kept his gun trained on Gamboori. Rather than worry about good faith negotiations, the henchmen opened fire as soon as Furii came into sight.

She memorised the scene in seconds. All four men chose to spray and pray as she ducked. Bullets still punched through the soft tissue of her left arm, but she had avoided anything that might end her immortality. Cursing quietly, she considered using one of Vincenza's pods, but that would vapourise Gamboori as much as his captors. She needed time.

'So, why let me go initially to try to kill me now?' Furii asked, reloading her guns and narrowing her focus. She had to screech over the din until they all had to reload.

'I wanted to see how much you knew about the autophages. Plus, the special request from the Duchess needed someone expendable.' The sheriff shouted back, revelling in his win already.

'Why me for that little genocidal joint venture?' Furii asked as she palmed her sickles. There was one advantage to having this moment in a small room.

'Let's face it- if you killed them, it was a win for us. If they killed you, it was a win for us.'

'Dead if I do and dead if I don't, huh? Lucky I am already dead then.' Furii shouted as she kicked off the wall, vaulting across the small room to run and flip on the adjacent wall. Using her trajectory over the stunned deputies, Furii sliced off their heads and faced down the remaining two. They paused in shock at seeing the heads of their peers thudding on the plush carpet, and Furii took that chance to leap between them and remove another two heads. That only left the sheriff, who was already turning and running into the room behind. Desperate to end this, Furii launched the sickle in her dominant hand at the sheriff, but it merely thudded into the door frame.

He had run, and soon heated voices blared from the next room. Furii ignored them while she cut the cable ties securing Gamboori's arms behind his back and retrieved her blade. She handed him two spare guns and a few explosives as she instructed him to get Isabel and prepare the truck to leave.

He was smart enough to not argue.

Time to kill the sheriff and cleanse the world of the Duchess who owned him. Furii fully expected more armed men and was not disappointed. The next room was a massive entertaining area, filled by men bristling with guns. These were the Duchess' men, her personal guard. Each had a feral look in their eyes and top of the range weapons. The hapless sheriff stood in front of them, clearly not by his own personal will. Piss ran down his leg as Furii launched herself at him wordlessly, planting the blade of one sickle into his chest and dragging it to his skull before he could even think to raise his gun. Furii held no pity for the sheriff as one of the main puppeteers.

The men all dropped to a crouch, guns aloft and fingers pulling triggers. Furii used the Sheriff's corpulent body as a shield to progress further into the room and waste some bullets. The few that penetrated through thudded off her armour, having lost all of their momentum within the rotund corpse. She threw what remained of him into the men on her left, while she thew herself at the ones on the right. Sickles bared, she kicked off the chest of one man to propel herself both into the air and into a spin. This allowed Furii to easily lop heads with a sickle in each hand, decapitating two and slicing well into the forehead of another.

The bodies dropped and she landed on them awkwardly, making her tumble down with them. She cursed loudly as one of the others got a shot off, the projectile managing to sneak its way into her vulnerable side. Furii felt the bullet punch through her ribs and deep into the lung. She scrambled to her feet and assessed the situation. The men on her left had recovered and were beginning to point guns in her direction. The survivors on the right were already shooting, bullets pummelling the gold flocked wallpaper around her. The Duchess was gonna be pissed about the state of her mansion.

Furii cussed again as one of the stray bullets tore through a chunk of her cheek. Bone splintered and flesh flew with the momentum of the lead. She worked quickly to decapitate the remainder of those on the right side.

There was no mercy for the mercenary types hired to protect the Duchess in her army. They were as callous as she was and would likely be the ones charged with hunting Furii down after the escape. Better to thin their numbers now.

More meaty thwacks indicated her success with maiming and removing limbs. Furii had no time to draw breath, however, as the cronies on the left side were now shooting earnestly while reaching for assorted other bladed weapons. Another bullet managed to skip through her armour and toured her right arm before exiting. Furii cursed in pain but was surprised to feel that they were not silver bullets. Either the Duchess skimped on the ammo, or she did not trust her own hired army. Fed up with being shot, Furii opted to just turf one of the explosive pods into the middle of the squad. She launched herself to the furthest distance from the bomb, courtesy of the nearest grunt. The mercs seemed oblivious to the tiny terror amongst them. In seconds the room was filled with a red mist, and body parts were raining down.

Furii had let the blast flatten her against the wall, then rag-dolled with the air current. This ensured she survived, albeit with plenty of bruises and at least one thing broken. Most of the mercenaries were now hanging in the chandeliers- well, pieces were. Some of the giblets were embedded into crevices of her armour, while the rest had made a Jackson Pollock piece of the walls. Furii fished a few extra blood caps from her stash tin, the last she had on her. Still, it was enough to encourage her blood loss to slow and bone shards to knit together a little.

Limping into the next room gave Furii enough time to change weapons, holstering her sickles to equip a fuller gun. This one at least held silver rounds, although shooting it with both arms seriously wounded would not be fun. Her blood still sluggishly dripped to the floor from all her wounds.

'Duchess, don't play coy, come on out and chat with me. I promise it will be worth the effort.' Furii's voice was low and grim, promises of pain dripping from every syllable. There was a nervous sort of shuffling in the next room, hushes and whispers. Furii smirked. This was not the behaviour of trained mercenaries.

She booted the door open, relishing the crunch of expensive wood under foot. There they all stood, various members of the vampire elite, decked out for a soiree. They truly must not have believed Furii could take out that many men. The shock turned to fear as Furii scanned the room to look for her quarry.

Unfortunately, the Duchess was planning for this, rising quickly to run out another door. As Furii raised her gun and shot, she was bumped in an odd sort of tackle. Her shot went low, hitting the Duchess in the thigh. The seedy little man who had tackle-bumped her was now quivering as he held a gun up at Furii. She laughed at the mother of pearl handled, short barrelled six shooter he pointed at her chest.

Such a scene was comical as she raised her own gun once again, cordite still spewing from her last shot. Her blood had mixed with it and dripped a violent brew from the tip of a beast that dwarfed his pop gun. Worst of all, she smiled. Calmly, slowly, smiled.

'Do you really want to do this, impotent little man with an impotent little gun?' she drawled slowly. That leg wound would slow the Duchess Du Mort enough for Furii to indulge in some intimidation. The man simply quivered on the spot, so Furii viciousy pushed him back and watched his scrawny legs buckle. 'If any one of you gets another idea to try to step in, just remember who dismembered the almighty Duchess' army, and how dead that will make you, cowering here without any protection.' Furii took the time to aim her hand cannon around a little, just to drive home the point. She really did not want to have to use it. Killing any one person from these families might make them band together and hunt down her newly liberated humans and self.

When they all nodded and held up empty hands, Furii began to moved on. A small pop went off, and a bullet thudded into the back of her helmet. She whipped around and shot the only fool holding a weapon, the scrawny legged man who had apparently found his feet and courage. His head rained down on the fancy clothes of the guests in bloody ribbons. Shards of skull struck the other guests, but other than expressions of pain, they did not dare risk antagonising the hunter. The body slumped to the floor without a single word from any of them. Furii shrugged.

'I warned him, warned you all.' Again her audience nodded with hands aloft.

Beyond the soiree room there was a short hall, but the trail of noble blood led into a study. Furii saw a flash of her gaudy party dress disappearing into the rows of bookshelves. She was so close to retribution.

The Duchess was limping into a small panic room, but Furii had prepared for this. Of course, a noblewoman of the Duchess' status had a panic room. Of course, she would abandon everyone in favour of saving herself. As the massive, reinforced steel door came down, Furii skidded two of Vincenza's excellent pod explosives under it, one to each side of the room beyond. As the door sealed tight, she heard the muffled thwump of the detonation.

Anything inside the room would be vapourised by now. It must have been an expensive panic room, as the door showed no sign of damage under the pressure of such intense explosives, nor did any smoke leak out. The Duchess Du Mort was wallpaper now. Furii sniffed and began her own slow, painful limp back to the truck.

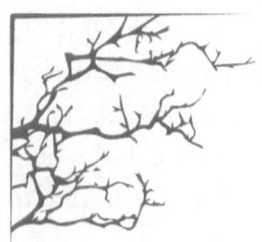

Chapter 19

After she had cleared the majority of the rooms with only minimal slips in the blood slicking the floor, Furii could finally see freedom. The side door was before her, the night seeped in and promised she could slip out into the shadows.

Some deity decided to piss on her parade, however, as a weak battle cry rang out. The damned snooty butler came at her with a silver sword, embedding it deep into her shoulder from behind before she could react. The severe loss of blood had made her slow. Furii slumped forward, pulling herself off the sword and face planting on the floor. *At least the humans had a chance to escape. Isabel would see to it.*

How they would get through the gates of the citadel would be a challenge without her, but Furii felt comforted. The clicky heels of the butler snipped closer, ready for a finishing blow. She waited serenely, before the serenity was shattered. Gunshots rang out, brain matter rained down. Isabel grabbed Furii by the shoulder of her armour and dragged her out of the mansion as the headless body of the butler dropped to the marble. Furii was blacking out as she was thrown into the back of the truck by the little autophage. Somehow Isabel had the power to lift and throw a heavily armoured and muscled vampire in her spindly little limbs. She had retained her raw autophage power.

Isabel instructed the humans to begin to treat Furii's wounds as she slammed the armoured doors closed. Stalking to the driver's seat, Isabel slapped her wig on, cursed it out the second she did, then jumped in. The truck started without complaining, despite the bullet wounds it too had suffered. The autophage floored the beast, slamming aside the sheriff cars in her haste to get back out of the driveway. The humans didn't dare complain, simply held onto all they could fins as purchase. Gamboori held Furii's shoulder together, but she had lost too much blood to heal, and was losing more by the second. She was near unconsciousness, and dangerously close to the true death.

Gamboori shivered. He knew she desperately needed blood, but the Duchess had abused them all with it. Pain, fear, death had all come with many of her feedings. Hesitantly, he held out his arm.

Gamboori's heart beat a fearful tattoo, growing ever greater to Furi's perception. It filled her senses in a terrifying manner. The predator within her stirred and uncoiled. Its tendrils poked at the edges of her mind, testing the borders of her sanity. The blood song in his veins called for Furii. It beckoned, with promises of solace and satisfaction.

Her wounds were so deep, every jolt of the truck tore through them. His arm was so close, to just tear into the tender skin. Violence flashed in her eyes, fed by the fear in his.

His arm was offered. Freely. Trustingly. Furii took a shuddering breath, then bit down carefully. Her saliva quickly numbed the area, and released the calming agents and euphorics that came with the right kind of feeding. Furii had kept control despite the hunger within, fanned by the automatic will to survive.

Gamboori relaxed, completely taken over by the chemically induced daze. His heart slowed; his jaw slackened. Furii fed, but pulled short of taking her fill. To do so would kill him, and probably at least another two humans. She held back, with her instincts screaming to continue.

Gamboori looked surprised.

'How... why was it like... that?' Gamboori stuttered and stumbled over his words in his haze of hormonal tranquillity. His bite had even stopped bleeding. The other humans gathered around, grabbing at his arm and sharing his surprise. The bumps in the road made it difficult.

Despite still being extremely low on blood, Furii registered their confusion.

'Wha you mean? Is vampire ven'm. Freaky good times for bitey,' she slurred. Her head lolled around with weakness but at least her shoulder was holding together.

Gamboori grinned deliriously before lifting his shirt to show his torso. Scars of savage tearing marred every part of his chest and stomach. Clear bites were present, but they then showed long strips where extra flesh was torn away. Knife slashes and even fingernail wounds crossed the entire mess. Many of the other humans lifted shirts or sleeves to reveal the same. Furii could barely get her eyes to focus, but she got the gist.

'S ok. Made 'er wall paint fer yeh.' Furii gave a weak thumbs up as she spoke. The humans all nodded, then looked up front as Isabel threw the door between the cab and the back open.

'Hold on to something guys, they won't let us out. Time to get tough,' she shouted back as shots rang out. The humans grabbed what they could and huddled around Furii.

'She gonna break my truck.' Furii argued as she tried to sit up and stop the ride. It was too late, Isabel had already floored the vehicle and soon pounded through the checkpoint and gate. Road gave way to desert and the truck kept going.

'Phew! Glad those reinforcements held, or you would have been real mad, hey?' the little autophage chuckled with adrenalin giddiness. Furii mumbled about her heart, but the humans were too distracted by the sight of desert stretching off into the night. They were in awe, many of them not having seen the outside world. They chattered excitedly, but with an undertone of fear still present. They had the tiniest hint of freedom.

Gamboori smoothed down Furii's hair and brushed some dirt off her cheek gently.

'Thank you. For keeping your word and showing us all some good in the world.' Furii tried to listen, but sleep was already closing in on her, needing more than blood to heal from this one. Thanks to Gamboori, she might actually wake up.

Isabel drove until dawn prickled the horizon, then handed over to one of the humans who had managed some sleep. They had all agreed to manage their shifts so there would be no need to stop. The autophage tiredly climbed into the back, carefully closing the door to prevent any sunlight getting in. She grabbed out the many blood caps Furii had bought and dosed out extra for each of them. Furii took them gratefully, then eased back to sleep the day away with Isabel beside her. Gamboori stretched out on the other side, having spent so much time protecting the others that he had forgone sleep himself. The three slept peacefully, safe together.

Furii woke to whispering. A conspiratorial huddle had developed by the door.

'We could just open it now and they would be ash. Get 'em before they know what happened. Before we get devoured by them.' There were whispered agreements as hands reached for the door handle. The humans were plotting to let the sun in, and it was too late for Furii to do anything about it.

'Felice, plotting to kill our saviours is a good way to lose the faith of the rest of us.' Gamboori growled, trying his hardest to be commanding, but not wake up the others. Felice and her plotters muttered quietly and slowly backed away from the door. They did at least have the dignity to look guilty. Furii let out the breath she had been holding in a raspy sigh. Many of her wounds were improved, but her body had suffered so much damage it would take days to heal. She wasn't actively bleeding, but the bones of her shoulder had not even reattached yet. The arm hung as limp as a dying flower. Should they have opened the door, there was nothing that Furii could have done but burn.

Gamboori looked sadly at Furii and Isabel, who had blessedly slept through the attempted murder. His eyes were almost obscured by dark shadows, the weight of someone with little sleep and too much burden.

'Sorry. Everyone is a little on edge. Well, defensive. It's been a nightmare.'

'Hey Gamboori. You once said there were over 200 humans in that building. Here we only have around 15. Where are the rest?' Furii asked tentatively. Now that she was more lucid, she realised that they had freed so few humans.

'From what the others have told me, many were lost to the Duchess' temper when I left. Then after I... returned, she took delight in killing many others in front of me. As a lesson, I suppose. That is why it was so easy to convince everyone to leave the second time. And why they are so vengeful.' The last part he directed to the conspirators still loitering by the door. They all averted their eyes in shame. Furii thought for long moments, at a loss for some kind of pithy platitude to soothe wounds deeper than flesh.

'I'm sorry...'

'Don't. That was the past, this is the future. We can heal, you almost gave your un-life for this chance.' As Gamboori spoke, the other humans began to nod in agreement. Furii realised she didn't know any of their names, but that would pass the time over the next few days as they fled to join the tribe. She looked down at Isabel. The autophage had saved her life yet again. The kid looked so peaceful, her skin now clear, silver hair springing from her head. She looked healthy. Furii took the time to watch her, embracing the serenity it gave.

The humans shared the food that was there for them, some exclaiming delightedly when they found things such as fruit. Apparently the Duchess fed her humans minimally too, unless she planned to feed upon them. Not even their excitement managed to wake Isabel. Furii looked on enviously as she slept unfettered. The gentle bumping of the truck lulled her into a calm trance but sleep eluded Furii.

Her reverie was shattered by sudden movement. Isabel was twitching violently in her sleep and emitting trembling yelps of fear. Finally, Furii opted to wake her gently, both for the sake of the others still attempting to sleep, and to stop whatever vicious and vivid terrors beset her. When she woke, Isabel was disoriented and weak.

'You OK, kiddo?'

'Just a lightmare.'

'Well you are safe here, go back to sleep.'

'Not a kid...' Isabel's mumbled complaints trailed off as she swiftly fell back into a dream-free sleep. Furii smiled and lay back down, praying for some sleep of her own to aid her healing.

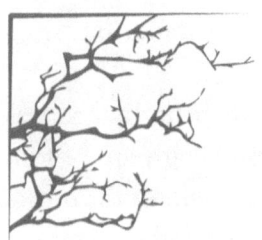

Chapter 20

Over the next days Furii came to know the name of every human on the truck, and even Felice began to like her. They kept moving constantly, travelling towards the rebellion base they had found Gamboori in. Each of them who could drive took it in shifts to do so. Many times Furii felt grateful for having the truck she did, the beast could just keep running without stopping or needing to refuel. Without knowing it, she had invested in the perfect getaway vehicle for this exact moment. Especially now that she had no comms pod, and therefore no identity to the system. Furii had thrown it from the truck after taking a convoluted detour, before running it over. There was no way she would allow anyone from the city to track her via the pod. She was truly jettisoned from the city and all it brought. The idea still invoked fear into her core, but she kept it to herself. Instead, she looked over at Isabel and Gamboori.

'What next? We meet up with Nakhari's tribe tomorrow, then where do we go?'

'Well, you didn't see the whole of the facility that I was living in. To be honest it could probably fit and feed an entire tribe.' Gamboori offered. Furii tilted her head in confusion, an adorable move for a living weapon.

'There was only one room we really didn't check. I knew we had you. But there was no real food or anything there. It was nice but would not do for all of us. Especially not the tribe. It was my fault they had to leave their lands.'

'Look, I am glad you didn't go through into that area as it's where they hid the children too, but there is so much more to it. Apparently, it was once an underground lab before the fall, used to preserve all kinds of plants, seeds and more. There is incredible experimental hydroponics gardens and water purification. It was supposed to help rebuild humanity if some kind of cataclysmic event occurred. There are kilometres of underground halls, farms and living spaces. But you must go through this hidden door. Well, two of them. With special ID cards. They are super old tech, but still work.' Gamboori was so excited about his description of the base that Furii couldn't interrupt his monologue. His face beamed with eagerness. It made her involuntarily smile, which annoyed her to no end. This human was starting to affect her.

'Well, it sure sounds like I missed out. Probably for the best, really. My orders were to annihilate everyone in the base. The Duchess and the sheriff were abundantly clear on that point. Aggressively so.' Furii responded, watching as Gamboori's face fell to sadness again. She felt every bit a monster. Why this human elicited such turbulent emotions was beyond Furii's current comprehension. Meanwhile Isabel was watching the whole interaction with the goofiest of grins on her face. Furii wanted to scream. To her insurmountable relief, Gamboori soothed frayed nerves.

'They are truly vile, but you probably saved a lot of wholly innocent people that day, humans and vamps. Those tunnels are full of non-combatants who are trying to hide and regain their strength or unable to. At least now we can keep the tribe safe too.'

'So where is your tribe? Nakhari mentioned you were not a part of theirs.'

'They... are dead. Or moved on. The Duchess told me I was neglected and abandoned as a child, but I hardly think that is true.' Gamboori seemed unwilling to elaborate further, so Furii dropped the subject immediately. The future had to be the focus.

She was also sick of making Gamboori miserable.

Instead she turned to Isabel.

'Tell me about your parents. How did you end up such a badass?' Furii asked carefully, hoping to elicit happier memories, not their death. Isabel broke out into a wide smile.

'They were amazing. Initially they were feeder humans, and part of the night guard. They wanted to have children, so they dedicated all of their time and money to me and my sister. We were so happy together, but one night we had a late comer. One of the nobles came into our home illegally. We didn't know who it was, but we know it was a noble because there were a large amount of guards out the front. The bastard gorged himself on my parents first, saving me and my sister for dessert. My sister was so close to death when he finished, then he freaked out. Instead of being blamed for murdering humans, he infected us instead. Somehow, he felt that taking the choice from us about immortality made up for actual mortality. Whatever the logic, we were left there, infected and confused, while he disappeared into the night with his entourage.' Isabel paused to reflect a moment, gathering the threads of a memory over 100 years old. Furii and Gamboori waited patiently, unwilling to interrupt her.

By this time the humans who were listening in had now also gathered in a small semi circle around Isabel, fully invested in her tale. Even the stubborn Felice had scooted over to sit up the back. Some even brought snacks to hand around.

'We were scooped up in the morning when they saw signs of a break-in and thrown into vampire rehab. We were fed, healed up and sent on our merry way. Unable to continue working as day guards, my parents were head hunted by a bounty hunter clan. The training was intense, and as my sister and I were now perpetual teenagers, we decided to join as well, to earn our own way. We trained and studied our hearts out, becoming a bounty hunting family. We were most effective. It was... heaven. My parents, my sister and I, our lives had changed so much, but we were together. Of course, the investigation of our infection resulted in nothing, but we were even prepared to let that go.' Isabel stopped again, pretending to take a break. She knew that she was at an excellent tension point in the story telling. They had many kilometres to go, and a tale certainly made it faster. Furii again admired the way this kid could both wield a blade and weave a story.

'So, we worked our way up the ranks, and made a pretty penny, as all four of us shared a home with our individual incomes, et cetera. It was nowhere near what the nobles have, but we lived well. Then my parents were requested on a job for a noble. When they got their, the blood sang. The creation met its maker. Despite their acceptance of the situation now, my father could not help a response. The noble noticed; knew he had been identified. I suppose he never thought, despite our immortality, that one day we would be sitting in his foyer, a bunch of armed bounty hunters. I think he was actually more scared than anything else. He hit an alarm; his army came. We hit the ground, and they dragged us out. My father was the pacifist still, told us not to fight back. He trusted on the good nature of narcissists.' Again Isabel paused, drawing out the tale in fine form. She was relishing the attention, and the less murderous nature of their companions. She also stopped to accept a dosed-out hand of blood caps. No one was willing to risk the vampires going hungry in such close conditions.

'We were taken into custody, then handed over to the sheriff with no definition as to our crimes. They seized all we owned, bits, blood, property. The clan kept their silence, then we were dumped outside of the city gates. For a while we could still ply some trade around the city, but soon that dried up too, and we were forced to move into the wastes. Even then we managed to eke out an existence until the blood ran out and we lost the last delivery convoy. My parents turned into autophages first, then my sister. I guess I didn't really notice when it took me. I mean it felt gradual, but one day I turned around and realised I was grey. So, we all lived as this... they would find an occasional loose vamp or human and tear in, I would try to keep going on the scraps. They couldn't talk, but we all seemed to work in some way. I knew they were gone, become what we once hunted. For a while it felt like what we deserved. Then Furii dropped into my little enclave.' Isabel left it at that, refusing to cast judgement or anger over the statement. The other humans looked from one to another, unsure how to react. Seeing that Isabel remained calm, they slowly all began to nod, before dispersing once they realised story time was over. Furii and Gamboori stayed, consuming the thoughts that were turbulent from her story. There was no real need to speak, all knew, and each had taken their turn to reveal their darkest moment. The three of them were forever bonded by their pain, love and loss.

The rebel base hit the horizon before they encountered any real kind of danger. There was the occasional autophage that ran out to be crushed under the tyres, but nothing that looked like retaliation. The tribe was yet to make it there, relying on guiding beasts and ensuring none were left behind. Despite the cramped living space, they had all gotten along rather well. The fact that the humans got to try real food certainly kept morale up, along with the absence of Duchess-level violence.

There were no guards to attack as they approached the base this time. The truck was parked a short distance from the main entrance. Furii, Isabel and Gamboori jumped out first to check that it was not an ambush. The others were left safely locked in the truck, most too weak still to fight. Thankfully there had been no more talk of mutiny in the trip over.

The three of them walked grimly into the gates, causing Isabel to give a nervous chuckle.

'A vampire, an autophage and a human walk into a bar...'

This book was planned to be a stand-alone, however there is other adventures that may spawn from here. In the meantime, please enjoy the first chapter of Demon Desired, the first book in my upcoming The Bayton Agency series, to be released in Q1, 2025.

IF YOU HAVE ENJOYED this book, please consider giving a good review on Amazon or GoodReads. To authors, especially indie ones like me, it makes a huge difference. Word of mouth is also very important!

IF YOU WISH TO JOIN my ARC reader team or mailing list, please email me at Ysadora.alexander.author@gmail.com or on any of the usual social media sites at Ysadora Writes. You will know me by the lil' witch!

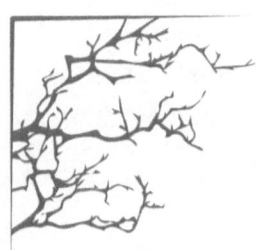

Prologue

His breath hitched in his throat. The one hunting him was so close. There was a dark pall over the already bleak night, and somewhere within stalked the one pursuing him. The glare of a predator had nagged him all evening, a lingering notion of a threat that he initially tried to laugh off. When in a full pub it was easy to do, surrounded by intoxicated friends and intoxicating women.

Now he was alone.

The street stretched into the gloom, the streetlights unusually absent. Sounds dulled, gone were the usual cars trawling for the girls whose steel heeled stilettos beat out a tattoo of the flesh trade. No bawdy songs or hacking coughs that narrated his usual walk home. Tonight, it had all dissipated into a miasma of fear. He ran for the next alley, waiting for his eyes to adjust to the sudden darkness. There was a scratch, a sigh. A stench to overwhelm the senses. While he had hoped to hide out in this moist alley way, littered with the discarded refuse of a sex and drugs kind of town, it seemed to be already occupied. While the greasy illumination of a street light still flowed into the mouth of the alley, it barely penetrated halfway down the first wall. Despite the impenetrable darkness, he knew that there was a great many someones hidden beyond the meagre light. As someone stepped across the mouth of the alley and blocked his light, he knew he was trapped.

'Is this about my...' His final words were cut short with the blade of a knife and many grabbing, rotting hands.

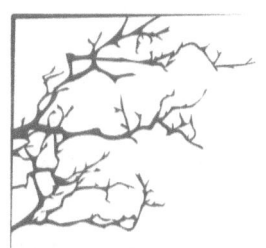

Chapter One

Tessa had never really been one to rely on her sensual nature, but if the time called for it, she could certainly play up on her best visual attributes. She stank of flowery perfume, rouged her cheeks and had even put on sheer pantyhose. The low-cut blouse on the other hand, that was a staple of her usual work attire, along with sky high heels. Fidgeting on the spot, Tessa began fluffing her already teased out hair, comforting herself mindlessly while she waited for those huge, intricately carved oak double doors to open and the interview that would change her entire life to start. Tessa had been an intern witch with the Agency for four years now, and now her future as a fully-fledged witch, an Agent, depended on how well she could schmooze the lurid, sexist pig in charge of her division. It was well known that he was loathe to promote a woman, although so far, he had shown a distinct weakness for a pretty smile and "lady-like" rose perfume. Now it was Tessa's time to play on that weakness.

The Agency had once had an official name, but it had long fallen into disuse as it didn't really have any competition. They were something of a police force, defending the innocent magickal beings and mundanes from the eviller witches and entities who needed to be... controlled. These were the necromancers, the hex casters, the magickal serial killers. The summoners of violent spirits and creators of foul magickal creatures. These offenders all fell under the Agencies jurisdiction. They were the final word on all crimes of a magickal nature. If a crime was clearly proven, the Agency were freely given the right to be judge, jury and executioner. Such was the fear of the mundane population when it came to magick as a whole.

The world of witches, demons, faeries and various other critters had remained hidden for millennia, however in the face of greater connectivity and media, as well as the rapid increase of technology, they were flung into the light. The only reason a genocide did not occur was due to fear. Several clever witches displayed great acts of power from a warfare standpoint, and in the face of an impending world war, various governments scrambled to launch a witch hunt. Not to persecute them, but instead to recruit them to their cause. From the attack force of the winning side, as well as the secret witches' counsels, came the Agency.

The Agency was a hierarchical and bureaucratic mess, while holding the reins were the oldest witching families and their incomes. Nepotism was popular, but for all its flaws, the Agency was entirely a necessity. It also offered an opportunity for eligible young people to escape their various circumstances, which is what Tessa had done. Some of the poorest kids in Bayton had managed to escape the gutter thanks to a magickal aptitude.

Teenagers who had any real kind of magickal skill were taken into the Agency while young and trained intensely as interns. They were guided by mentors within the Agency, and often saw their mentor as surrogate family. When deemed ready, the kids were thrust into the world as full Agents, witches of the law. Interns made very little money, as all the bonuses for a job well done went to their mentors, despite it generally being the interns who had done all the legwork. The intern system was a joke, but it was one of those "bureaucratic system" things that had never progressed from the 1950's. Regardless, Tessa had made it through her various trials and was ready for her final assessment. Unfortunately said assessment was the responsibility of the heads of each department. While they had the mentor's notes, the supervisors had the final say of the careers of people they barely knew.

While she should get through on merit alone, a little flirtatious insurance never went astray. She clicked open her compact, hastily powdering her nose and checking her appearance one last time. Not stunning, but she guessed she could pass as a bit of a looker really. Certainly, she had never lived up to the standard that her mother had aspired. With her hair dyed as red as a cheap sports car and a smattering of freckles, Tessa would almost be cute if it weren't for the many tattoos and piercings. Sure, many of the tattoos were of the magickal sigil kind, the traditional markings of her profession, but they were interspersed with plenty of pin up girls, sugar skulls and the occasional XXX poison bottle. Dressing to kill, complete with liberty rolls and swing skirt was the best way to get by when you lived on the edge, in the Bayton city slum.

Somehow in the wake of all the destruction and desolation of the old world, a thriving rockabilly and punk scene had sprung up in the previously gentrified areas, and Tessa was more than happy to indulge. Living solely on an intern's meagre wage meant she had no real choice in the matter anyway. Bayton was a sleazy little city, but it was a sleaze she knew well. It was a sleaze that fit like a couture glove. She was at her most comfortable in this world.

Nearby a stern throat cleared, breaking Tessa out of her reverie. Sir McAdams was leering over her, probably hoping to catch a better view down her shirt. How he got those enormous doors open so quietly she will never know. Clearly, he was mighty stealthy for someone his size, a hint of the Agent that was. She snapped her compact shut and threw it in her bag before rising as sensuously as she could, although she felt more akin to a newborn giraffe attempting to stand.

Her sensual efforts must have been at least a little effective, the Sir's eyes were now bugging out of their red, watery rims as his puffy face reddened. It was a repulsive, blobby, sweaty mess.

Why was it that all sleazy men seemed to have red watery eyes, she mused as she tottered into the office, *was it because they all stare at anything with a hint of cleavage far too much? Did it cause some kind of permanent damage?* Distracting herself with such inane thoughts would not help her with what was to come. She had to focus. It was time for a little game of make believe.

Tessa perched on the edge of the offered chair as the Sir hefted his putrid bulk around the desk, ungainly throwing himself down in a sweaty heap. His shirt tails poked out of his pants, stained with many past meals wiped from his hands. His tie was the elasticated kind, and had seen too many sweaty board meetings given the way it hung loosely, with elastic long perished. Filthy glasses sat low on his nose and a wet bottom lip hung lower. Sir McAdams was a caricature of a man, the personification of middle management. How he had ever been a field Agent was a popular subject of postulation by the interns. He cleared his throat again, perhaps attempting to look wise, and began to leaf through what Tessa assumed was her employee file.

'Contessa Bale,' he murmured as Tessa flinched. Her mother had big dreams and a poor sense of humour when it came to naming her bouncing blond bundle of joy. Imagine her disappointment when Tessa became an Agency witch rather than a trophy wife. Not that she hadn't jumped on the opportunity when the official Agency examiners had come to her school. It was finally a chance at a future which interested her more than the tedium of being a pretty wife to a rich man. Protecting innocent magickal people and mundanes who had no skills at all was dangerous work, but the idea had thrilled Tessa. Being a member of a rich mundane family had never satisfied her, and when the Agency's tests came around no one expected her to pass, let alone pass with skills that were above the contemporary testable power levels. It was her ticket out of there and she grabbed it with both hands. Who cared that she lived in the slum area of Bayton, that her car barely ran, and the neighbours were less than desirable. To Tessa that just made them more real. She was eternally thankful to have won the genetic lottery of being born with magickal skills. Sir McAdams coughed again and leafed through a few more papers, to what end she had no clue. Somewhere in the middle-management script was "make them wait."

'Contessa, you are here to be assessed as to whether you are ready to be deemed a fully qualified and registered witch of the Agency are you not?' he said, in a thin voice that was attempting authority but getting lost in the slime. She nodded, before working to get her own voice to resonate with those dulcet tones usually favoured by phone sex line workers and other talented strumpets. It felt like she was trying to talk through thick molasses.

'Yes Sir, if I am worthy...' She almost choked on the effort of forming the words thus, but the quick tug of the collar indicated that her ploy had worked.

'Well Contessa, you appear to have an exemplary record, while working under your mentor your capture or kill rate has been outstanding. The mentor's notes are good, Lady Marique has indicated you handle yourself well with matters both magickal and mundane. No innocent or mundane loss. Yes, yes quite the record.' Tessa fought the need to roll her eyes; thus far the Sir's own eyes had done more wandering of her body than her record. Although, that was the idea.

'I believe I am ready Sir,' she said, batting her eyes, hopefully coquettishly, although the overall effect was probably more comparable to having a seizure. Sir McAdams sniffed, waving a hand idly. Clearly that slight challenge to his authoritarian decision was undesirable.

'I will ascertain that. However, your record is good. We do have more cases than available and competent witches right now so I shall allow you to go through. Hereby you shall be known as Lady Bale, an investigator witch of the Agency with full powers of the law both magickal and mundane.' With those final words Sir McAdams puffed out his chest with self-importance, magnanimously bestowing this gift of a bigger pay packet and nondescript title. He reached for a red folder from the top of the stack of files that permanently littered his desk.

'You will be honoured to know we have already assigned you a case. The details are in here, something to do with goings on in the area you live I believe. Take it now, any research you need can be done in the Halls. Report to Lady Kirk in order to get your restricted spell items also, along with the witches' sigil.' With one last leer Sir McAdams turned away, reviewing the folder of what Tessa assumed was the next interviewee. Those simple words and that was it, she was an indoctrinated witch. She muttered a thanks and grabbed the folder, fleeing the sense of being pawed at and undressed with the sweaty pervert's eyes. While she exploited the sleazier men in her life when it was necessary, it didn't make her feel good after the fact. Perhaps a shower in bleach, perhaps some steel wool, perhaps some industrial cleaner, then she would feel more at ease.

The Agency had something of a hierarchical system, indoctrinated witches were called Sir or Lady to delegate their rank above that of an intern. There were also the Sibyls, who had the dual role of being on hand seers and admin staff, as well as the Elders who had done their duty in the field and survived. The Elders were rather rare, and greatly revered. The Elders were cared for until the day they died at the Agency, such was their value. The advice of the Elders was greatly sought after by the Agent witches, and the Sibyls often attended the Elders for insight on what they had seen.

This system was both flawed and seamless. Initiation rituals were done when an intern was approved to join the Agency. It was a ritual and legal binding, full of spellwork and paperwork. The actual success rate of interns making it to a full witch was relatively small, although luckily death was rare. It was far more likely that an intern would drop out, something Tessa had considered many times. Her mentor Lady Marique had been stern, and many of the other interns had been terrified of the fierce woman. Tessa had welcomed her nature, as it came with an unconditional support. Plus, she didn't particularly care for fitting in with her fellow interns. Many had come from the well to do, rich witching families that controlled the Agency, and had the personalities and work ethic to match. Being born to a mundane family and living in the slum meant that Tessa was a pariah, ostracised from their inner circle-jerk. Her few friends she did have were considered the deviants and weirdoes, those forced to live at the Agency.

The halls of the Agency were oddly busy, so it took Tessa quite a while to squeeze her way through the loiterers and head to Lady Kirk's... repository, for want of a better word. Part storehouse, part tattoo parlour, part impromptu therapy clinic, it was the go-to for all Agency witches, where they got all necessary magickal ingredients for spells or the latest magickal sigil carved into their flesh. Tessa loved these rooms, where the heady scent of herbs and dried animal parts drifted over the subtle disinfectant used for the tattoo area. Rich wooden shelves of magickal accoutrements and loose herbs at one end, autoclaves and stainless steel at the other. Lady Kirk was not busy for once, keeping a shrewd eye on a few young Sibyls digging through the yarrow and mugwort. She greeted Tessa warmly. With an open face surrounded by a shock of greying hair, Lady Kirk was agelessly stylish. Her unusual amber eyes were framed by cat-eye glasses. With a fondness for brightly coloured kaftan style dresses, Lady Kirk was a glorious burst of vibrancy in the drab Agency halls. Her prominent tattoos were equally bright, which Tessa loved to see on an older woman. Lady Kirk was all bright smiles and musical laughs.

'Finally a witch, my dear! Ready for the big wide world?' she said, teasing gently in her soft voice that had always calmed Tessa. This time the new witch allowed herself the luxury of rolling her eyes openly.

'Sure am Lady Kirk, Sir McAdams was his usual self! What have you got for me?'

'Ugh, that man! Did you know that a year ago he...' her voice trailed off as she realised the Sibyls had stopped their rummaging and were now listening intently. 'Uh well, yes you will be needing your full witches' sigil and a kit, just a few things on top of your basics. Let's get to the tattoo first and you can tell me all about it!'

Tessa grinned and gave her a thumbs up. Witch tattoos were not like the mundane version, instead of traditional ink a blend of willow bark and sage ash was used, much like the old primitive scarifications. This combination was sacred because it stored the magick chanted into it at the time of tattooing better. The witches' sigil was one of both power and protection, while also being a rather nifty form of ID as they sat dead in the centre of the chest. Lady Kirk did the best work around, and Tessa had always found it a pleasure to be tattooed by her.

The sigil was done in no time, and with very little pain thanks to the buzz of magick that came with it. The Sibyls had finally left with their pilfered goods, leaving Tessa and Lady Kirk alone to peruse the shelves of the restricted section.

'Seeing as they are throwing you straight into a case, we better get you set up with some nutmeg, musk and ylang-ylang for a truth charm... OH and you definitely need wormwood, dandelion and willow bark for a demon summoning, they are just far too useful. Probably some black iron, cascarilla and orris root for a bit of extra protection and some althea to boost your psychic skills to detect magick in a pinch. That will do for a start, but come and see me if you need anything specialised, OK?' Lady Kirk grinned as she threw each item into a sealed bag, as well as a few sneaky extras.

Tessa was about to thank her and leave but the Lady grabbed her hand tightly. Her eyes were bright with tears. Tessa had never seen Lady Kirk so pale and unhappy.

'Please, don't forget to summon your demon with a pure mind, after last week I, I...' Her voice cracked as the tears rolled down her rouged cheeks.

Demons, contrary to popular belief, were not inherently evil creatures. Their nature depended wholly on the person doing the summoning, so aside from being slightly sassy, a demon summoned for a good purpose would generally be good themselves. They were incredibly useful, being able to detect all forms of magick, walk on other planes of existence as well as being very good physical and magickal protection. All Agency witches used them regularly, and after their task was complete, they were sent back to Hel.

Unlike the popular fire, brimstone and torture concept of Christianised Hell, Hel was just the afterlife for the dead and home for the demons. Many books had covered the subject of Hel, although it was all rather stale. Utilising demons in this way was a good arrangement for all involved, as demons could not exist on this plane without a human anchor. Some demons considered it to almost be like a holiday.

Unfortunately, last week a newly qualified witch had summoned a demon while angry about a personal problem and had unfortunately ended up in many tiny little pieces. Far worse for the other denizens of his apartment block, the Agency had gotten there too late to stop the wholesale slaughter of every person within reach. The surviving members of the Agency were all still shocked, but Tessa had to shake it off.

'I will be careful; I may not even need a demon this time. I might get lucky and have a really easy one, a pissed off faery or a magickal pick pocket!' Lady Kirk did not seem convinced at this, so Tessa just smiled confidently, packed up her kit and headed home.

SEE YOU AGAIN IN 2025! Demon Desired is coming in Q1!

www.ingramcontent.com/pod-product-compliance
Lightning Source LLC
Chambersburg PA
CBHW020655180626
46816CB00003B/1302

* 9 7 8 1 7 6 3 6 8 7 4 1 7 *